"I'm going to open the door and we're both going down the manhole," her new bodyguard told her.

"No!" Princess Isabelle attempted to free herself. Her royal motorcade was under attack, but that didn't mean she was going underground.

Levi had her clamped against him so securely she couldn't move more than an inch in any direction. She felt his neatly-trimmed beard brush her temple as he spoke briskly into her ear. "Once I open the door we'll be vulnerable. We need to get below ground as quickly as possible."

Isabelle took a shaky breath. To his credit, though he held her immobile, Levi wasn't squeezing her too hard for her to breathe. Maybe it was that small allowance that made her decide to trust him.

Or maybe it was because she didn't have any choice.

Another blast rocked the air, and the hood from another vehicle crashed against the limousine's windshield.

"We won't be safe if we stay here. We've got to move now."

Books by Rachelle McCalla

Love Inspired Suspense

Survival Instinct
Troubled Waters
Out on a Limb
Danger on Her Doorstep
Dead Reckoning
Princess in Peril

*Reclaiming the Crown

RACHELLE McCALLA

is a mild-mannered housewife, and the toughest she ever has to get is when she's trying to keep her four kids quiet in church. Though she often gets in over her head, as her characters do, and has to find a way out, her adventures have more to do with sorting out the carpool and providing food for the potluck. She's never been arrested, gotten in a fistfight or been shot at. And she'd like to keep it that way! For recipes, fun background notes on the places and characters in this book and more information on forthcoming titles, visit www.rachellemccalla.com.

PRINCESS IN PERIL

RACHELLE McCALLA

Love Inspired

Recycling programs
for this product may
not exist in your area.

LOVE INSPIRED BOOKS

ISBN-13: 978-0-373-67483-1

PRINCESS IN PERIL

www.LoveInspiredBooks.com

Printed in U.S.A.

The Lord says: Although I sent them far away among the nations and scattered them among the countries, yet for a little while I have been a sanctuary for them in the countries where they have gone. I will gather you from the nations and bring you back from the countries where you have been scattered, and I will give you back the land again.
—*Ezekiel* 11:16–17

To Genevieve the Brave, my princess

Acknowledgments

With thanks and gratitude to my husband Ray,
patient first reader, whose grammar and
spelling skills far exceed my own.

Thanks also to Emily Rodmell, visionary editor,
and all the helpful readers whose insights and
encouragement have helped to hone this story.
I hope you will not be disappointed.

And eternal praise and thanks
to our Lord Jesus Christ, hero of that great epic,
King of Kings and Lord of Lords, Amen.

ONE

The royal motorcade lurched to an unexpected stop. Her Royal Highness Princess Isabelle of Lydia glanced at Levi Grenaldo, her recently appointed bodyguard, expecting him to make some reassuring gesture that would indicate nothing was amiss.

He didn't look her way. In the silvery sheen of his mirrored sunglasses, Isabelle saw only the rear bumper of her brother's limousine sitting still on the road in front of them. The seconds ticked by and they sat, unmoving, in the narrow streets of Sardis, Lydia's capital city.

Something had to be wrong. The motorcade represented the power and pageantry of the royal family and therefore *never* stopped until it arrived at its destination.

"Why are we stopped?"

Levi didn't acknowledge her question, but instead pressed the button for the intercom and told the driver, "Get us off this street."

When the driver hesitated, Levi pressed the button again.

"Now."

Much as she wanted to remain calm, Isabelle felt her fingers tighten as they gripped the edge of the leather seat. She didn't like anything about this situation. For one thing, she didn't trust Levi.

He'd been abruptly appointed as her personal bodyguard five days earlier with no explanation given, and on top of that, he didn't fit the profile for a bodyguard. Although he was plenty tall and his shoulders were broad with muscles, he was otherwise trim, and the dark angles of his beard gave his face a scholarly look. Unlike all the bodyguards she'd ever had before, his neck wasn't thicker than his head, and he looked unusually sharp in the tuxedo he wore for the state dinner they were about to attend.

Besides that, the bodyguard read books. Intelligent ones. She'd seen him with his nose buried in political tomes whenever he waited for her to finish an appointment.

Out of place as those attributes seemed, what really bothered her was the way he overrode her requests and limited her freedom. As the eldest daughter of King Philip and Queen Elaine, Isabelle was used to having to change her plans to protect her safety, but Levi's impediments went far beyond the usual. They'd butted heads several times. After three days she'd asked to have him removed, but her father had refused her request.

All her instincts told her something was amiss.

The driver had the car two points into what promised to be an eighteen-point turn on the narrow street when suddenly a deafening blast rent the air, rattling the official limo, and an orange ball of fire seared the sky in front of them.

Levi's hand mashed the intercom button.

"Back! Back! Now!"

A second explosion rocked the air even closer behind them, and Isabelle felt the car shudder. Though the royal limousines were made of bullet-proof materials, she doubted they'd be any match for that kind of explosion. Her heart twisted with concern for the rest of her family. Alexander, her only living brother, rode in the limousine ahead of her, which didn't appear to have been damaged by the blast, but her parents' car was out of sight ahead of those carrying other royal officials. It would have been close to where the first explosion hit.

And her sister, Anastasia, rode in a car somewhere behind hers. Black smoke filled the air. Isabelle couldn't see any sign of her sister's car.

Levi cracked the door open and looked down at the street, letting in a wave of heat and the stench of fire and explosives.

"Shut that!" Isabelle lunged past him to close the door, mindful that, inadequate as the car might seem against the fiery blasts, it was the only protection they had.

He pulled the door closed and would have met her eyes had his not been hidden behind his ever-present sunglasses. But his face was suddenly far closer than she was used to her bodyguards' faces being, even in the midst of pressing crowds and certainly not in the backseat of a car.

His hand hit the intercom again. "Back up three feet and a little to the left."

The driver obeyed promptly this time.

Even before the limousine had come to a stop, Levi had the door open again. He leaned out and wrestled with something on the ground.

For a second, Isabelle thought about shoving him out and locking the door after him. But much as she didn't like the man, she wouldn't stoop to such a move just to keep herself safe, though his actions seemed to endanger both of them, and it frightened her.

A moment later he pulled the door closed again and slid back, slipping one arm solidly around her waist.

Isabelle gave a yelp and tried to jump away.

The vise of his arms didn't allow her to budge.

"Your Highness, I'm going to open the door and we're both going down the manhole."

"No!" She twisted her torso in an attempt to free herself.

Levi had her clamped against him so securely she couldn't move more than an inch in any direction. The touch of his hands and the tenacity of his grip sent memories scurrying out from the dark corners of her mind—memories she'd hoped to keep hidden forever.

She felt his neatly trimmed beard brush her temple as he spoke briskly into her ear. "Once I open the door we'll be vulnerable. We need to get below ground as quickly as possible. *Don't* fight me."

Isabelle took a shaky breath. To his credit, though he held her immobile, Levi wasn't squeezing her too hard for her to breathe. Maybe it was that small allowance that made her decide to trust him.

Or maybe it was because she didn't have any choice.

"The car is bulletproof," she reminded him in one last attempt to derail his plan. "We won't be safe if we leave it."

Another blast rocked the air, and the hood from another vehicle crashed against the limousine's windshield, the royal hood ornament visible for just a second as the dented metal scraped past them.

"We won't be safe if we stay here." Levi reached across the seat. "You can take your purse." He shoved the satin clutch into her hands. "Anything else you need?"

Isabelle tried to think, but her mind was filled with fears for the safety of the rest of her family. Judging by the proximity of the last blast, she was nearly certain it had been centered just ahead of Alexander's limo. That may have been the hood of his car that had fractured their windshield! She couldn't see anything through the black smoke, but she sent up a silent prayer and forced herself not to act on the instinct to leap from the safety of her vehicle to look for her brother. He was a grown man and a soldier. Surely he knew more than she did about staying alive.

"On three." Levi's words jerked her thoughts away from her brother and back to the crazy-sounding plan to leap through the manhole. "One, two—"

With no time to protest, Isabelle pinched her eyes shut as Levi opened the door and, in one swift movement, pulled her from the vehicle and shuttled her through the hole in the pavement. Much as she didn't trust him, she knew the danger outside was real, and she didn't want to be exposed to it any longer than was absolutely necessary. For that reason only, she cooperated with his actions.

She opened her eyes as the soles of her leather pumps slid against the slippery metal bars that formed a ladder secured to the wall of the tunnel. Although she couldn't get purchase on any of the rungs, Levi seemed to have a steady hold on both the ladder and her. She wished she'd chosen to wear something a bit more practical than a silk, floor-length evening gown, but the dress had been the perfect choice for the state dinner she was now about to miss.

Her trembling hands reached for the bars, and she managed to grip one securely.

"Hold on tight." Levi's instructions sounded close to her ear. "Got it?"

Unable to muster up words, she nodded. He surely couldn't see much in the darkness of the hole, but he must have felt her movement because he let go of her and reached above them to pull the manhole cover shut.

Metal grated against pavement and Levi's body rocked as he muscled the cover back into place above their heads.

Orange fire flashed above them and Isabelle felt its heat penetrate their hiding place.

Levi immediately let go of the manhole cover to shield her. As the simmering air stilled, he slid the manhole cover the last couple of inches closed, leaving them in total darkness. "Are you okay?"

Isabelle could feel herself trembling, but she forced her voice to speak. "Fine. You?"

"Fine," he echoed.

"You didn't scorch your hands, did you?"

"Not too bad."

Isabelle was aware that he hadn't denied being injured, but because he didn't complain, she didn't press the question. It wasn't as though she could do anything for him at the moment.

With the manhole cover blocking out all light, the darkness was damp and absolute, and Isabelle felt a wave of terror wash over her. Who was this man, and what were his intentions? What did the explosions above mean? And where were they? Her nose told her it wasn't the sewer.

"Can you climb down, Princess?" Levi's voice surprised her with its closeness.

Suddenly mindful of her position wrapped in the arms of a man she didn't trust, Isabelle resisted going any farther. Gripping the metal bar a little tighter, she ignored his prompt. "What was that?"

"Ambush." He stated flatly. "Let's get moving."

Isabelle reached upward for the next higher rung. "My family is up there. My brother's car—"

"You're *not* going back up." Levi tugged her back down, closer against him.

The grip of his arms in the darkness brought more horrible memories rushing back. She fought him instinctively. "No! I don't know who you are or what you're doing—"

"Your father hired me to protect you." Levi's arms

were too strong for her, and her position on the slippery metal rungs was a precarious one.

She tried to fight back. "The royal motorcade was ambushed and now you're trying to kidnap me. I demand to know why!"

Instead of responding, Levi wrenched her free of the rungs and climbed downward with her more or less slung across his shoulders. "We need to get moving. If the lid on this hole sustains a direct hit, you could be killed standing where you are."

"Where am I?" A shudder of fear chased through her, but Isabelle stopped fighting and relented to being carried down the dark hole. She felt the vibrations as another explosion rocked the earth in spite of the thick stone that surrounded them, so she didn't doubt Levi's warning was sincere.

"The Catacombs of Charlemagne."

Isabelle startled and nearly fell out of Levi's arms. He obviously hadn't expected her to jolt at his words.

"We're in the Catacombs of Charlemagne?"

"Yes."

"But they were filled in more than a thousand years ago." Her words, spoken in an awed whisper, echoed through the empty chamber.

"Your father had them excavated." Levi climbed downward, his movements slow and deliberate in the darkness.

"How do *you* know that, and *I* don't?" Isabelle couldn't fathom why her father hadn't told her. And how had Levi learned of them?

"I was just wondering the same thing." Levi's voice echoed louder, and Isabelle realized the chamber had widened with their descent. He continued. "Actually, your great-grandfather King Alexander III began the excavation during the first World War, thinking the royal family might need the catacombs to escape if they were ever threatened on their own soil." His posture changed as he let go of the ladder, and Isabelle heard the scraping sound of his shoes against the floor of the tunnel. "Little did your great-grandfather know, he was right—just a century off."

Isabelle wished she could see his face, but the utter darkness hid everything. So much had happened so quickly, she wasn't sure she entirely understood what Levi was talking about. "The catacombs run beneath the city of Sardis." She recalled from history lessons. "Charlemagne built them in the ninth century when he used Lydia as an outpost in his attempt to further his kingdom and the spread of Christianity toward the east."

In a patient-sounding voice, Levi continued the story. "Lydia has always been a Christian nation, so they supported Charlemagne's efforts."

"Even though he was eventually thwarted." Isabelle wasn't sure how large a space they occupied, but from the way their voices carried, she judged it to be at least a few meters wide, with a ceiling well above their heads. Tentatively she stepped away from Levi, half expecting to feel cold stone against her back. She felt nothing. With a shiver, she took a step back toward him, unwilling to lose her only human contact in the vast darkness.

"Stay near me." He cautioned her abruptly. "We need to get moving."

Isabelle gulped a breath of the cool underground air. She had to think. Too much about this situation wasn't right, and just because the man knew about the catacombs, that didn't mean she ought to trust him. After all, there was surely little coincidence between the timing of his appointment and the attack on the royal motorcade. For all she knew he was in on the ambush and had brought her into the tunnel to finish her off or hand her over to a political enemy.

But how could she sort out what to do when she couldn't even see?

Levi tugged on her arm.

"Hold on." Isabelle pulled her cell phone from her purse and flicked it open, illuminating the screen, its miniscule light startling in the utter darkness of the tunnel, casting their faces and the rock walls around them in an eerie greenish glow.

"Thank you. That helps." Levi offered her a slight smile.

To Isabelle, his angled lips looked sinister in the flickering light. "You should take your sunglasses off."

As she watched his face, his jaw tightened under his close-cropped beard. He seemed reluctant to remove the mirrored shades, which, together with the facial hair, hid his face almost completely. At his hesitation, Isabelle realized she'd never seen him without the sunglasses on, not even indoors. For a moment, she wondered why.

Then he slowly peeled back the lenses and she knew the answer.

Not everyone in Lydia had brown eyes, but the majority of the people did. The country was located west of Macedonia, where the heel of the boot of Italy split the Adriatic and Ionian seas. Most native Lydians, like the people of Greece and the rest of the Mediterranean region, had olive complexions, dark hair and dark brown eyes.

As Levi pulled off his sunglasses, she saw that his eyes were blue.

She couldn't suppress her startled gasp. If Levi wasn't Lydian, how had he come to work for the royal bodyguard? The law required every member of the Lydian military to be a citizen—and no one could serve as a royal bodyguard without first serving at least four years in the military. By what deception had Levi tricked her father into hiring him? And what was he planning to do with her?

She realized he still had hold of her arm, and she wished there was some way she could pull away and nonchalantly put some distance between them. But Levi remained close to her in their small circle of light. Fear found its way into her voice. "The royal bodyguard draws its team from the elite of the Lydian military forces. Only citizens of Lydia can join the military."

"I am a citizen of Lydia."

"How is that possible?"

"My mother is Lydian. My father is American."

Isabelle felt her eyes narrow. Was he baiting her? Her father, King Philip of Lydia, had married an American—her mother, Queen Elaine. But it was a rare combination, and she found it doubly suspicious that she and Levi had something so unique in common. "Who do you work for?"

"The Lydian government." Impatience flickered in his blue eyes. "We should get moving."

"I don't trust you."

His expression relaxed slightly. "I sensed that. If you will agree to keep moving, I will explain a bit more of who I am and what I know of this afternoon's attack."

Isabelle's mouth opened slightly as she weighed her answer. Should she move farther into the darkness with this stranger? Every warning bell inside her clamored against it. Yet really, what choice did she have? Surely only danger waited above them.

"Where are we going? What about my family? They were up there in the motorcade—"

"We can't do anything to help them now. You have a responsibility as a member of the royal family not to endanger yourself, correct?"

"Yes." Isabelle felt her shoulders droop with resignation. How many times had her parents reminded her of that fact? Every time she left the country— every time she'd ever tried to do anything on her own. Even her humanitarian work overseas was often hampered by her royal obligation to her own safety.

"Then you can't go back up. We can only go forward." He looked down at the dim light from her cell phone. "We should save the battery. Close that—we can walk in darkness."

A protest rose to Isabelle's lips, but she doubted it would do her any good to voice her fears. Levi was right about the light. There was nothing more for it to illumine—just the stone walls of the catacomb, and they could feel their way along those well enough. Surely the light would become more urgently necessary in the future. He was wise to advise her not to waste it.

She snapped the phone shut and the light went out, leaving them in total darkness again. "Explain, then. Who are you? And what just happened up there?"

Levi cupped her elbow with one hand. In the total

silence of the tunnel she could hear his other hand skimming along the wall as they moved cautiously down the cobbled floor. The blue-eyed bodyguard began his story.

"My father works for a Christian organization called Sanctuary International. Their primary mission is to help religious refugees find asylum. Thirty-five years ago, when he was working in the Balkan region, he formed close ties with your father. Lydia is one of the few countries in the region where religious freedom is zealously defended, and your father proved to be an invaluable ally.

"During that time, my father and mother met and were married, but they returned to the United States before I was born. I received dual Lydian-U.S. citizenship through my parents, and though I was raised in the United States, I often spent summers visiting my grandparents in Lydia."

Levi paused. "The wall curves away," he murmured, "and I suspect it forks."

Before he finished speaking Isabelle had her phone out, and its tiny light illuminated the two branching tunnels gaping open in endless darkness. The bodyguard glanced between them before nodding. "This way." He didn't hesitate to step forward down the right-hand branch.

"Why this way?"

"After two more turns we will be below the Sardis Cathedral. It should be safe to exit there."

"How do you know the catacombs so well?" Isabelle closed her phone reluctantly, still suspicious of his motives in spite of his story.

"I've been studying them for the past six days."

"Why?"

Levi seemed to struggle with how to answer her. Once again, Isabelle's suspicions were raised. Was he really who he said he was? Did the history he told her really happen, or was he simply making it up to placate her until the rest of his nefarious plans could be accomplished?

His answer seemed to come in a roundabout way. "Our aid workers in the region have formed close ties with many Christians with diverse political ties. Six days ago, an informant delivered a coded message at a Sanctuary outpost on the Albanian border. The next morning his body was found floating in the Mursia River."

Isabelle found that her steps had slowed as she listened closely to Levi's explanation. "What did the coded message say?" She shivered a little as she stepped tentatively through the darkness, uncertain whether she really wanted to know the answer to her question.

Apology and regret filled Levi's voice. "It contained instructions for an attack on the royal family."

"Today's attack?"

"Presumably. It did not give a date or time. That's why I immediately replaced your usual bodyguard."

"I don't understand."

"The message was supposed to be delivered to Alfred, the man who was scheduled to guard you today. He was apparently a member of this insurgent organization. The message contained instructions. As soon as the first explosion detonated, Alfred was supposed to kill you."

TWO

Levi didn't like sharing the details of the planned attack with Isabelle. He didn't want to cause her any more distress than she'd already experienced. But because she didn't trust him, he didn't know how else to impress upon her the gravity of her circumstances. Whether she trusted him or not, he needed her to follow his every instruction. Their lives would depend on it.

Now the princess stumbled and Levi held her arm more firmly to steady her.

"Alfred?" Isabelle repeated, disbelief in her tone. "He's been part of my guard for four years."

"I know, and a member of the royal army for sixteen years before that. We have been unable to determine when he joined the insurgents."

"Where is he now?" Isabelle asked. "I should hope he was arrested and questioned."

"He was floating in the Mursia next to the man who brought us the message."

"Yet the insurgents still went through with the

attack? If they knew enough to kill those men, they had to have known the note was intercepted."

Levi could only guess at what their original plans might have been. "Perhaps they thought the longer they waited, the more time we would have to prepare a defense."

"But if my father knew about this, why did my family stay in Lydia? Why didn't we leave the moment the message was intercepted?"

With his head bent a little closer to hers in the darkness, Levi wished he could study the face of the princess entrusted to his care. "Surely you know the answer to that question."

A resigned sigh was Isabelle's only indication of emotion. "My father would never leave the throne. It would signal to the insurgents that he was a coward."

Levi nodded. "They would see it as an open door to walk through and take the country."

"Then why weren't my brother and sister and I at least sent away? Why were we all in the same motorcade?"

"The three of you were originally supposed to be riding in the same car," Levi reminded her. "Your father refused to call off the state dinner for the same reason he would never run away from his throne." Levi had begged the king to send his children away for their own safety, but he understood King Philip's reasons for keeping them there. They had argued about it well into the night. Levi was still exhausted from missing sleep.

Now he answered the princess patiently. "Your father believed that, with the message intercepted, the insurgents would change their plans and call off their attack. He feared that if he tried to send you away, they would see it as a sign of weakness and instead attack with greater force. He thought this would be the best way to keep you safe."

Isabelle trembled. Levi realized that, on top of all that had happened, the damp cold of the catacombs was probably getting to her. With only narrow straps instead of sleeves, her dress surely did little to keep her warm.

As her regal posture sagged under the weight of all she'd absorbed, Levi slid off his tuxedo jacket and nestled it around her shoulders. He, too, feared for her family and what may have happened to them. She had surely guessed their fate, and Levi had no reassurances to give her. There was really very little hope for the Royal House of Lydia.

"We should keep moving," he said softly after her trembling had given way to sniffling. "If we can reach other Sanctuary team members, perhaps they will have good news about your family."

"Maybe I should try calling them."

Levi sucked in a breath.

"Why not?" Isabelle pulled back from him.

"We don't know who would answer your call, and

we can't risk the wrong people finding out where you are. For the same reason, I have no intention of using my phone until we reach a safe location. If Alfred was working for the insurgents, anyone could be." He urged her on. "The best thing we can do right now is get you out of here."

The princess took several deep breaths but made no move to head forward.

"You still don't trust me?" he asked.

"I trusted Alfred."

Levi nodded. "Perhaps you are wise not to trust me." Her long hair, which had been piled high in an artful arrangement for the state dinner, had come loose, and a thick strand brushed his hand. "Can you open the light?"

She clicked her phone open, and her wide brown eyes stared fearfully up at him in its thin glow. Gently he pushed the loose hair back from her eyes.

"Your hands were burned," she accused him as his fingers passed through her line of vision.

"I hadn't meant for you to notice," he apologized. "There is nothing we can do for them here."

The princess straightened, as though drawing from a well of courage only a royal could tap. "Then we must get to a first aid kit. Let's hurry."

Levi took her cue and turned them down the next tunnel, which would lead under the centuries-old Cathedral where many Lydian saints were buried. The church had been built upon the rumored burial place of the original Lydia, an early leader in the Christian church whose conversion by the Apostle Paul was detailed in the sixteenth chapter of the Book of Acts in the Bible. The nation of Lydia had been named for her house church, and the royal family, including Isabelle herself, could trace their roots back to Lydia's family.

It was a reminder to Levi of the amazing lineage of the woman who held their only light as they walked through the darkness of the catacombs. Though he had long respected Isabelle from afar as he'd read about her humanitarian efforts as a princess, he was even more impressed with her in person. And she was even more beautiful than the newspaper photos he'd seen.

"Which way?" Isabelle asked when they arrived at the next fork in the tunnel.

It was a good question. Levi had studied handdrawn maps of the tunnels, which were known only to a select few. Because King Philip had supplied the maps, Levi had assumed the whole royal family would be familiar with the layout of the catacombs. It surprised him that Isabelle was unaware of their very existence. Now he tried to recall the detailed twists and turns of the elaborate underground labyrinth.

The light from Isabelle's phone dimmed. "Do you know which way it is?"

Finally able to picture he map in his head, Levi

pulled her a little closer to him as they headed down the left-hand passageway. "This way, but let's leave the light off if we can. We might need it more later."

To his relief, Isabelle didn't argue with him but shuffled along beside him as they made their way down the tunnel in dizzying darkness. He could only hope she would cooperate with him for as long as it might take to get her to safety. Their situation was difficult enough, and Levi desperately needed the mission to be successful.

Not only did he care about his mother's home country and feel allegiance toward the Royal House of Lydia, but he also had a very personal reason why the mission could *not* fail. His father didn't just work for Sanctuary International, he was its president. And he'd be retiring in another year. Everyone expected Nicolas Grenaldo to appoint one of his two sons to be president after him.

And that was just the trouble. Although Levi had spent four years in the Lydian army before going on to law school, he didn't have any battle experience. He'd studied international law, thinking at the time it would give him the best possible background for leading an organization that helped people throughout the world. Too late he'd realized no amount of studying would earn him the respect and admiration of his peers within Sanctuary.

His little brother, Joe, however, had spent six years in the United States Marine Corps, followed by several successful and high-profile operations with Sanctuary. Joe had saved the lives of dozens of missionaries, political figures and refugees over the years.

Levi had saved no one. As the older brother, he should have been the natural choice to follow in his father's footsteps. But as of right now, Joe was everyone's favorite. Joe was a hero. Levi desperately needed this mission to go well if he wanted his father to see him as anything other than a scholar. And for that to happen, he'd have to have Isabelle's cooperation.

The darkness was so complete it made his eyes hurt. Levi had almost begun to wonder if he'd missed the stairs when a gap in the wall left him grasping into the open air.

He stopped.

Isabelle snapped her light on just long enough to display a twisting set of stone stairs that curled upward and out of sight. Then she let the light die again before stepping forward onto the first stair.

"Wait," Levi whispered, tugging her back. "We need to discuss our next step."

As he pulled her back, she brushed near him, and this time, with her standing one step higher on the stone stairs, he felt her lose hair brush past his cheek and smelled her flowery fragrance, so different from the dank catacombs. He swallowed, refusing to allow himself to think about how close she was to him.

Levi had always known Isabelle was a beautiful woman, but he was in her life for a short time only, to fulfill a specific mission. He would behave with absolute decorum. She was, after all, a princess. And he'd been briefed privately by her father about the horrors of her failed engagement. Sympathy and respect stifled his otherwise-strong sense of attraction toward her.

She must have realized how close she'd gotten to him in the darkness because he felt her back away. He doubted she felt anything near the kind of attraction he did, but then, she'd already said she didn't trust him. Perhaps it was best that way.

"What is your plan?" Isabelle asked.

He could feel the warmth of her breath on his cheek and realized she hadn't backed too far away from him after all. Still holding her arm with one hand, he analyzed their options.

"We don't know if the insurgents are aware of the catacombs or of the opening below the cathedral. I would assume not, but—" He hesitated.

"I would assume nothing, under the circumstances."

Levi agreed. "We'll make our way up the stairs in silence. I've never been through this way so I don't know what we'll find at the end."

"Is it even passable?"

"Yes. Your father wouldn't have allowed it to be marked as an exit if it wasn't passable. But because we don't know if it's a sealed door or if your light will show—"

"I'll keep my light off."

"Good. Given the possibility of danger ahead, we can't risk giving away our presence."

"Extreme caution." Isabelle concurred, and he could feel her head nod in the darkness.

Levi was acutely aware of the slight movement. She'd slowly allowed herself to lean closer to him. Did she realize how close to one another they now stood in the dark chamber? He tried not to think about his proximity to the princess.

The pressing danger provided excellent distraction. "We'll proceed with extreme caution," he echoed. "If at any point we encounter any person or anything that seems out of the ordinary, we'll halt and assess the situation. If danger is apparent, we'll retreat back the way we came."

"And if we cannot retreat into the catacombs?" The princess tipped her head forward as she spoke, and Levi felt the softness of her hair come to rest near his jaw.

Levi didn't feel he ought to push her away, yet the floral perfume she wore teased his nostrils. "Then God help us."

Isabelle pulled back from him.

The cold air of her absence cleared his mind.

He realized how his words must have sounded and rushed to explain. "We don't know the size of the forces the insurgents have attacked with. If they take the cathedral and block our passage to the catacombs, then it would mean they've completely overwhelmed your father's government, in which case I don't know how we could possibly get you out of the country alive."

"Out of the country?" Isabelle backed farther away from him this time. "You said my father didn't want me leaving the country, that it would send the wrong message to the insurgents."

"That was before the attack," Levi corrected her. "You can't expect to stay—"

"I will not leave!"

Levi's hand flew out to cover her mouth. "Shh," he hushed her, aware of how loudly her voice had echoed. She squirmed away from him. He hadn't intended to clamp his hand over her royal mouth, but he couldn't risk letting her voice give away their location when they didn't know who might hear.

Cautiously he removed his hand.

Isabelle whispered angrily. "You said my father wished to avoid any sign of weakness—"

"They think you're *dead*." He tried to reach for her shoulder to pull her back so he could reason with her, but she batted him away. "Princess Isabelle." He spoke her name with caution.

"The Royal House of Lydia is not dead. We live and we reign."

Levi was reminded by the emotion in her words that she'd been raised with a profound sense of duty toward her people, an obligation of leadership that had been deeply ingrained since birth. It wasn't in her to run away when her government was challenged. How could he make her understand that she *had* to do just that?

"Yes." He spoke in the most soothing voice he could muster. "Yes, Lydia is ruled by your family, by the Royal House of Lydia."

"I am *not* dead," she choked.

He realized she was weeping. He didn't blame her one bit. "You're not dead," he repeated, trying to think of what he could possibly say that wouldn't make her more upset. What was there to say? It was likely the rest of her family had been killed. She had surely guessed that much already. As soon as the insurgent forces realized she had escaped, they'd come looking for her. But he couldn't tell her that—not now—so he tried to reassure her as best he could.

"You're not dead, Princess. You're alive, and I will do everything in my power to keep you alive. But right now we don't know what the situation is out there. If the insurgents have taken control of the city—"

"No!" Isabelle moved to push past him again. "No, they *cannot* take the city." She turned as though she was going to stomp right up the stairs and demand to have rule returned to her.

"Isabelle." He pulled her back against him and this time held her tight so she couldn't do anything rash. He pressed his mouth near her ear as he had in the car and spoke calmly but forcefully. "The insurgents want you dead. As long as they think they have already killed you, they won't come looking for you. If they learn you're really alive, they'll hunt you down. Your only hope for survival is to stay out of sight and get out of Lydia as quickly as possible—before they have time to search for your dead body and wonder why they can't find it."

"But the Royal House of Lydia has never given over control of the country. It is my royal duty—"

"It's your duty to stay *alive*." As he held her tightly, he felt some of the fight leave her. "You can't reclaim the throne if you're dead. If you let me get you out of here, we can negotiate your rightful return to the throne."

"How can I run from my people like a coward?"

"Your only other option is to face near-certain death. Who will defend your people then?"

He felt her war with that decision as he held her, his arms still firmly rooting her in place lest she suddenly take off up the stairs.

Finally she told him in a determined voice, "I still don't trust you."

"It doesn't matter if you trust me. All I ask is that you allow me to protect you."

A huff erupted from her nose, and her chin lifted off from where it had come to rest on his shoulder. "Have I made it that difficult for you?"

"You did seem determined to stay in the car long enough for the insurgents to hit it."

"If you would have told me about the catacombs earlier—"

"I didn't know you didn't know," he defended. He relaxed his hold enough to let her move half an arm's length away but no farther. He still didn't trust her any more than she trusted him. "There may be moments up ahead when I don't have time to explain everything. Whether you trust me or not, you need to follow my lead. If I have to stop and argue with you at every turn, it will give the insurgents an unfair advantage. I fear we must move very quickly."

Her shoulders rose and fell under his hands as she took a deep breath. "Up the stairs in darkness, through the cathedral and then what?"

"The U.S. Embassy is across the street. They should be able to help us get out of the country."

Isabelle was silent. Levi could tell she was weighing her response. Based on the background information he'd been given, he could guess at what might be the cause of her silence.

"I know you don't care for the American ambassador," Levi began.

"Stephanos Valli remains in this country solely to retain the good will of the American government. If it were up to me, he would never be allowed to set foot in Lydia again." Her words seethed with barely repressed anger.

"We need the Americans to help us get you out of the country alive. If Valli was headed to the state dinner, it's likely he won't be anywhere near the embassy. His staff can get us out of the country." Levi had never met Stephanos Valli, but he understood that the American ambassador had Lydian ancestry and ties to the most powerful people in their area of the Mediterranean. Valli had negotiated the engagement of the princess to one of those people, a billionaire businessman named Tyrone Spiteri. The engagement had ended in scandal. Levi had never been told the details, but he understood Isabelle's bitterness toward the ambassador for his hand in such an embarrassing experience.

And Isabelle obviously wasn't ready to risk an encounter with Valli, though it had been two years since her engagement to Tyrone Spiteri had ended. "I have many friends who could possibly help us," she suggested.

"Do you know them better than you knew Alfred?"

She tensed, and Levi could feel her head shaking regretfully in the darkness.

"I suppose," she whispered softly, "we can't trust anyone because we can't be sure of whose side they're on."

"The Americans should be trustworthy."

"Perhaps." For a moment she sounded overwhelmed, but she seemed to draw quickly from that royal well of strength. "Let's get moving then. I still intend to find a first aid kit if we can."

Levi was impressed with how quickly she made up her mind and how silently she made her way up the stairs. He counted seven, eight, nine steps before his head knocked into something solid.

"Stop," he whispered quietly as a breath while moving to shield her head.

His burned fingers were momentarily squeezed between her high-piled hair and the obstruction. Tears sprang to his eyes but he stifled an exclamation. Finding her ear beside him, he whispered, "There's an obstruction above us. It may be a trap door. I'm going to try to lift up."

He eased his shoulders up against it, but even when he began to apply greater force, nothing budged.

"Does it have a latch of some sort?" Isabelle whispered back. He could feel her hands skirt past him in the darkness, and a moment later he heard a soft click. "Try it now," she whispered.

This time when Levi applied pressure upward, the ceiling moved silently, though the space above seemed to be just as dark as the tunnel they'd come from. With only a slight rustle from her evening gown, Isabelle slid through the opening, and Levi followed after her, closing the door softly after they were both out.

Isabelle's hand traveled up his arm, and he felt her fingers tug on his earlobe. At her prompt he leaned down and she whispered silently into his ear. "Should I try my light?"

Feeling for her hands, he covered the light, then nodded. "Go ahead."

The light came on and slowly he allowed more of its miniscule glow to shine. The two of them looked around at the statues and marble plaques, their blank-eyed stone faces deeply shadowed.

Isabelle shivered at the sight of the stone faces, whose forms hid the ancient bones of her ancestors. "The mausoleum," she whispered. They'd toured it once when she was very young, but no one had been buried under the cathedral in several generations, so she'd had no cause to visit it again. Her sole impression was that it was a frightening place cluttered with dead upon dead, which seemed to go on forever.

But then, she'd been only about eight years old when she'd made that tour. Surely it wouldn't be so frightening now that she was twenty-four.

Her light dimmed, and she snapped the phone

shut again. Although complete darkness shrouded everything from her sight, she was acutely aware of the looming stone figures and tried not to imagine their blank eyes staring back at her through the darkness. She had to remember that the insurgent threat against her was far more real than her fears of the dark and the dead.

"Do you know your way around in here?" Levi asked in a hushed whisper.

"No. Do you?"

"I've never been down here before."

"I visited once, but it was a long time ago. All I really remember is..." The memories stumbled through her mind, tripping over themselves like the patent-leather shoes she and her sister had worn as they traveled hand-in-hand through the tour, nearly running in the end, chased by fear, wanting only to find the sunlight. She stepped instinctively closer to Levi, the only human figure in the room who lived and breathed. "I didn't like it."

"Do you know which way we should go?"

Isabelle searched the long-buried memory, sorting through the fright to find some tidbit that could help them. "We came in through the back of the church and came out at the front. The mausoleum runs the length of the cathedral, with family crypts branching off on either side." She pulled his tuxedo jacket more tightly around her. "Most of these bones are more than a thousand years old. No was has been buried here in generations."

"So we should try to find the central hallway?"

"That much shouldn't be difficult. Then we go one way or the other. The trick will be not to get sidetracked, or we could end up wandering around here—" Her voice broke off as she heard a distant boom, the first sound to penetrate the deathly stillness.

"The trick will be to avoid detection." Levi's words were spoken in a near-silent breath by her ear.

Isabelle also tensed, listening to the sound Levi had obviously heard. Distantly, echoes reverberated through the still air. Footsteps? And muffled voices.

"Search every corner." The command rose above the sound of footsteps—many sets of footsteps. Someone was in the mausoleum looking for them!

Isabelle grabbed Levi's arm and whispered, "What are we going to do now?"

"The footsteps are all coming from the same direction. We need to run the other way."

Isabelle raised her hand to open her phone again and light their way, but Levi's fingers quickly closed over hers.

"No. No light."

"I can't see where I'm going." Isabelle protested in near-silence as Levi tugged her along beside him.

"No light," Levi repeated. "It will lead them straight to us."

They shuffled forward, and Isabelle couldn't help but wonder if they weren't leaving a trail of footprints for their pursuers to follow. But tourist groups went through the mausoleum several times a week, if not several times a day. Hopefully their footprints would blend in.

For a few moments they bumped along in darkness, here and again meeting the rounded sides of cold stone statues or the walls themselves. Then Isabelle's peering eyes were shocked as the bulbs that ran along the central hallway illuminated.

"They've turned the lights on," she whispered softly, her words nearly drowned by the echoes of boots on stone floor and the muffled shouts of the approaching men.

Because the branching crypts weren't lighted, she turned toward the light of the central hallway.

Levi pulled back on her arm. "They'll see you."

"But we're sitting ducks in here. There's no way out of this chamber unless we get to the main hallway."

Already the boom of footsteps pounded closer. She didn't know how thoroughly the men were searching the sprawling chambers, but they were closing in on them.

"We'll have to hide."

Isabelle looked around. The life-size statues were almost big enough to hide behind.

Almost.

"Where?"

Levi's fingers grasped the edge of one of the many marble slabs that rested on the raised ledges of the burial chambers. Isabelle watched as he slid back the solid stone slab.

"In here."

The boom of footsteps echoed nearer.

"No." Isabelle shook her head. "Not with the bones."

Levi pulled an object from the vault. "They're not bones." He held out an ancient piece of wood for her to see.

"It's a shuttle," Isabelle realized. She recalled from her long-ago tour that the burial chambers were interspersed with vaults containing items important to the deceased. Since weaving and textile work had long been the basis for the Lydian economy, many weavers treasured their looms and shuttles—even to the point of being buried with the objects that had been an integral part of their livelihood.

Realizing the chamber Levi had opened didn't hold any bones, she relented to hiding inside. Levi guided her feet-first through the opening.

"Hurry!" he encouraged her as the echoing footfalls drew closer.

"Did you hear that?" A deep voice echoed down the corridor.

"This way!"

The boom of boots on stone grew louder and faster as the men hurried toward them.

With a repentant gulp, Isabelle ducked into the hole, regretting that her hesitation had wasted precious seconds.

"Up ahead!" the men's voices called, nearer this time. Almost upon them.

Isabelle shuffled her head around so she could look out of the opening. Levi's face flashed across her line of vision. "Are you coming in?" she whispered.

"No time," he mouthed, shoving the stone slab nearly shut, leaving her with just a slice of light before he spun around.

THREE

Levi ducked instinctively as the bullet ricocheted through the stone chamber. He gripped the shuttle he'd pulled from the chamber, its ancient wood petrified with age. It wasn't much of a weapon, but it in the enclosed space it would be far more useful to him than the gun in his holster.

"Don't discharge your weapons inside the mausoleum!" The commanding voice Levi had heard earlier now sounded like it was just around the next corner. "The bullets could bounce back and hit one of us."

The sound of footsteps drew nearer and flashlight beams danced through the relative darkness of the side chamber. Levi leapt back, hiding in the shadow of a large statue nearest the opening of the chamber on the side from which the voices approached.

He gripped the shuttle as the footsteps boomed nearer.

The instant a shadow fell across the opening Levi

leapt forward and struck with the petrified rod. The man crumpled to the floor with a hollow groan.

"What—" The next soldier stepped forward, and Levi hit him, a glancing blow across the back of the head, which appeared to stun him only slightly. He grimaced and gathered himself, but Levi caught him under the jaw with his other fist. He slumped over his fallen comrade.

Two down. How many more to go?

With a shout, another solider leapt over the two unconscious figures. Levi swung with the shuttle, but the man's hand clamped his wrist. A high round kick cleared the two motionless men below them. He caught his attacker under the ribs.

He heard the air rush from the man's lungs as the soldier leaned forward, his grip easing on Levi's wrist.

Jerking his arm free, Levi caught the man in the back of his head before he straightened.

Just in time.

The soldier went down as another leaped forward. At the rate he was going, Levi would soon have the entrance to the side chamber blocked by the unconscious bodies of his attackers. This soldier's feet hadn't yet hit the floor when Levi caught him under the chin with a grunt, with the same motion heaving his body onto the growing pile.

He panted, trying to catch his breath. His singed

hands stung. How many more soldiers were there? How many more could he hold off?

The crackle of a radio told him someone was about to give away his position.

Vaulting the heap of men, Levi knocked the radio from the man's hand before the soldier could call in reinforcements. Grabbing his head by the helmet, Levi rammed the man face-first into his knee.

Three soldiers were still standing.

The nearest one spun sideways, clipping Levi in a blow to the chest.

Levi grasped the shuttle with both hands and brought it down on the man's head.

The soldier shuddered and went down.

"Alec?" The next guy looked at him in confusion.

Levi didn't recognize the young man. "Sorry," Levi apologized as he slugged the soldier across the jaw.

Before he had time to pull his arm back, the next man was on top of him, knocking him flat. Levi just managed to catch himself enough to avoid hitting his head too hard against the stone floor, but he wasn't quick enough to avoid the blow aimed at the side of his head.

Stars flashed across his field of vision, obliterating all else. Levi shoved back, trying to push the man off of him, to roll sideways, anything. But he was exhausted from what had already been a long fight against overwhelming odds, and this attacker was enormous.

The man on top of him had every advantage.

Levi braced himself and prayed.

Suddenly the man shuddered, falling on top of him.

With a whoosh, the weight of the oversize soldier knocked what remained of Levi's breath from his lungs.

He groaned as he attempted to heave the dead-weight figure off of him.

A small, neatly manicured hand appeared, hefting the man by the shoulder, adding just enough lift to allow Levi to push the man off to the side. As his vision cleared, Levi looked up to find Princess Isabelle smiling down at him.

"How did you—?" he started to ask.

She held up another shuttle like a royal scepter. "There were two of these."

Levi moaned and sat up. "But how did you get the stone rolled back from the inside?"

Motioning with the shuttle, Isabelle imitated how she'd levered the shuttle through the opening to move back the stone. "Simple tools," she said, glancing back at the heap of men behind her as a groan rumbled from the bottom of the pile. "We should get out of here."

"Sure." Levi leapt up and, with a quick kick in the direction from which the groan had come, muttered,

"That should keep him quiet." He plucked up the radio that had flown free when he'd knocked out the man who was trying to use it. "Let's go before anyone else realizes what just happened."

Isabelle hesitated. "Do we want to take their guns? We don't want these guys to be armed when they wake up—especially if it takes us a while to get out of here."

Although he didn't want to waste the time it would take to do so, Levi had to admit Isabelle's idea was a good one. The men could very well awaken before he got the princess through the cathedral and safely across the street to the American Embassy. "Okay, but let's be quick about it."

Levi grabbed the guns, stuffing several of them into the vault where Isabelle had hidden, before closing the stone seal. He then hurried to empty the soldiers' pockets of anything that might be useful before slinging an assault rifle over his shoulder.

Isabelle grabbed a flashlight from one of the prone figures. "These men are Lydian soldiers. I might have thought they were after me to protect me if they hadn't fired a shot at us." Her features clouded. The soldiers had betrayed their vow to protect the royal family.

But why?

Much as he didn't want to think about it, he knew the question needed to be voiced. "Whose orders were they following?"

Concern filled Isabelle's face. "As king, my father is the head of the Lydian military, but if any of the commanders had turned—" Her words broke off, the situation clearly catching up to her.

"Someone issued a command for these soldiers to come down here looking for us."

"Do you think they knew who they were looking for? Every soldier takes a vow upon enlistment to serve and protect the royal family. They must not have known they'd been sent after me."

Levi sensed her struggle as she considered what the presence of the soldiers meant. Did the soldiers know who they'd been sent after? He didn't have time to sort it out.

"We need to get moving. These men could wake up any moment."

With the bright lights shining down from the hallway ceiling above them, they ran the length of the hall, finding the door to the stairs still open where the soldiers had entered.

"Do you think it's safe?" Isabelle asked in a breathless voice.

Levi listened carefully but heard no sound above them. "I imagine the men were dispersed in teams to search the area surrounding the ambush. The cathedral is only about three blocks from where the motorcade stopped. It will take them a while to canvass the area. I doubt anyone will come back to this building until they realize our men downstairs haven't checked in."

"I hate to think they'd be organized enough to make that realization very quickly." Isabelle's intelligent eyes looked up at him intently, her loose lock of hair tumbling down and brushing his hand again. He doubted she was even aware of it, yet it did terrible things to his focus.

Her determined expression took his breath away. He knew she was shaken by all that had happened—she'd wept not very long ago—but here she was, already dealing capably with the situation. And she'd saved his life with that shuttle.

He swallowed, struggling to think what to say next. What had they been talking about? The woman was far too beautiful. As soon as he got her to safety he'd hand her off to someone else. She was difficult to work with—for all the wrong reasons.

Before he could gather his scattered thoughts, Isabelle surprised him by scooping up one of his singed hands into her much smaller fingers.

"Before we go any farther, we should pray," she said softly, pinching her eyes shut and bowing her head without waiting for a response from him.

"Lord God, Protector of Lydia, Sovereign of our Nation and Lord of the Universe." In her royal way, she began with God's majestic titles before pleading for protection—not just for them, but for the rest of her family. "Wherever my parents and siblings are, I know that You are with them. In Your infinite mercy, watch over them. Keep us all safe until You bring us together once again. Amen."

Levi also offered an amen and half expected Isabelle to linger after her prayer, but she didn't even look at him before she headed through the doorway. It took Levi another second before he realized he would have to hurry to keep up with the woman he'd been hired to protect.

Isabelle proceeded as quickly as she dared up the stone steps to the main back hall of the cathedral. She knew the way to the front entrance, having worshipped regularly at the ancient church since she was an infant. Not only did she want to make up for the time they'd lost already, but she felt the need to stay ahead of Levi. He'd begun to make her feel uncomfortable.

She was used to having bodyguards. They'd gone everywhere with her all her life. They were a part of her life.

But she'd never prayed with one before, never clung to one like she'd held on tight to Levi as she'd fought him, cowered in fear with him and wept with him.

Sure, she was plenty used to bodyguards. But she wasn't remotely used to getting that close to a man—any man. The very thought made her recall the final terrified minutes of her failed engagement.

Tyrone's face popped into her mind—the face of the man she'd wanted so much to love, the man who had only wanted to take advantage of her.

The hard-learned lesson dug itself a little deeper into her heart. She hadn't even suspected Tyrone's true motives until it had almost been too late. Tyrone had been in love with royal power. He'd wanted to marry her for the prestige it would give him.

Her desire to be loved had blinded her so much that she'd almost let him get away with his evil plans. Almost. She would never allow herself to make the same mistake again. She was a princess. Any man who pretended to love her was likely only in love with her royal title. Tyrone hadn't even taken the time to get to know her.

And she'd learned better than to waste her time chasing after love. She shrugged off the unfamiliar feeling of closeness that praying with Levi had caused her to feel. It meant nothing. As soon as she got away from the insurgent threat, she'd figure out how to get away from Levi, too.

They made their way quickly down the ancient stone hallway, which was slightly more worn than the floor of the chambers below but otherwise remarkably similar. Light from the setting sun streamed in through the beveled panes of the antique windows, prisms of vibrant colors splashing them as they ran past.

They reached the front doors, and both of them crouched back against the solid wood, peeking through the clear panes to the scene outside.

The cobbled street and limestone walls looked innocent, as though nothing out of the ordinary had happened in Sardis that day.

Isabelle watched as Levi's hand settled over the door latch.

"Do you think it's safe?" she asked, watching his bearded face carefully.

He pulled his sunglasses from the inside pocket of his tuxedo jacket as she handed the garment back to him. It would be warm outside. "Safer than in here. The front door of the embassy is less than one hundred meters from where we stand. We'll have to get down the cathedral stairs and up the steps of the Embassy, but we should be able to do it in well under a minute, maybe even thirty seconds if we hurry. That's not long for us to be out in the open."

Isabelle swallowed. "Front door to front door then?"

"That seems like the most expedient route." The mirrored lenses of his sunglasses stayed trained on her face as he slipped on his jacket. "You don't like the plan?"

He could read her that easily? "I don't like the idea of entering Stephanos Valli's turf, even if he's not there." Although three years had passed since Valli had engineered her engagement to Tyrone

Spiteri, and two years had gone by since the horrid ending of that engagement, the mere thought of seeing the two-faced ambassador brought her fears and anger back to the surface.

Levi extended one singed hand toward her arm. "I won't let Valli get near you," he promised.

Could it possibly be that simple? Isabelle looked down at the hand whose mere contact with her arm imparted a surprising level of comfort. "We never found any burn ointment for your hands," she realized with regret.

"It's okay. I've made it this far." His hand stayed still on her arm, and Isabelle wished she could see his eyes behind his sunglasses or his face behind the dark outline of his beard. He leaned a little closer. "We should get going. Are you ready?"

Isabelle nodded, clinging to Levi's promise not to let Valli near her. As long as she knew she wouldn't have to face that awful man, they could get to the Embassy and be safe. Finally.

Maybe then she could learn what had become of her parents and siblings. At least she wouldn't have to fear for her life anymore. And she could get away from Levi, whose presence had started making her uncomfortable for all sorts of new reasons, mostly because he'd gotten so close to her.

She straightened and mentally prepared herself for the dash across the street. "Let's go."

"On three," Levi announced, his grip tightening

on the door latch. "One, two—" The door swung wide and the two of them burst out, darting in a dead sprint down the steps.

Levi kept one hand on her arm and one hand on the assault rifle he'd lifted from the soldiers. Her heeled pumps offered little in the way of traction, so Isabelle felt grateful to know Levi was ready to catch her if she slipped.

They crossed the street in six strides and Isabelle hoisted the floor-length skirt of her gown as they vaulted the Embassy stairs by twos and threes. Levi swung open the front door and they stepped inside onto the glossy marble floor.

Isabelle looked up, expecting to see the usual uniformed guards that protected the embassy. Instead, Lydian soldiers guarded the entrance. The one nearest her smiled broadly.

"Princess Isabelle, what a pleasant surprise." He and the soldier next to him stepped forward, reaching for their guns. "If you'll hand us your weapons, we'll personally escort you in."

"We'll keep them," Levi said, his presence close behind her reassuring.

Something was wrong. She could feel it. There shouldn't have been Lydian soldiers guarding the door. There shouldn't have been Lydian soldiers in the building at all. Everything felt wrong. Scurrying soldiers stopped as they passed in the hall. What were Lydian soldiers doing in the American Embassy?

Another man in uniform approached them. "You've captured the princess?" he called to his comrades. "Valli will be delighted."

No! Terror squeezed Isabelle's heart as the two guards lunged toward them, their hands stretched out to take their guns.

Levi spun around her, stiff-arming the men in the face with the butt of his rifle before sweeping his other arm around her waist and scooping her up as he shoved his way back through the door. Out of the corner of her eye, Isabelle saw the other officers rushing toward them, pulling out their guns. The heavy doors slammed shut behind them.

Instead of heading back down the stairs and across the open street, Levi surprised her by scooting to the side of the marble landing and leaping over the balustrade into the bushes, taking her with him.

Prickly branches grabbed at her dress as she fell, but the moment her feet hit the firm earth, the branches settled above their heads. Levi shuffled sideways under the cover of the lush Mediterranean foliage.

Above them on the landing she could hear the doors bang open and soldiers shouting, wondering aloud where they'd gone. "Down!" Levi whispered, ushering her toward a window well deep behind the shadows of the landscaping.

Isabelle gulped a breath and jumped. Levi landed

silently beside her and immediately grabbed the window by its frame.

"What are you doing?" she whispered, more than aware that the Embassy building was crawling with Lydian soldiers, who were apparently reporting to Valli. "We're breaking back *in?*"

"Shh." Levi pulled the aging window frame from the time-warped wood. "You said you'd trust me."

A blur of responses passed through her mind, most of them involving their near capture moments before, but she bit her tongue and ducked, mindful of the darkness and the cobwebs. The stone room was similar to those in the basement of the cathedral, but instead of bones, it housed cluttered piles of old furniture, discarded desks and slumping stacks of boxes. Levi slid through the window and landed beside her, reaching back up and pulling the wood-framed glass into place behind them.

"Where are we?" She pulled his ear as close to her lips as she could so she wouldn't have to speak above the sound of a breath.

"The basement of the Embassy."

"You brought me straight into the hornets' nest?"

"I'm keeping you alive." He raised the assault rifle in front of his face, covering them as he moved toward the door. "Everyone is outside looking for us."

"So where are we going?"

"The last place they're going to look."

His words were ominous, and Isabelle swallowed, following him down the dark hallway. Unlike the underground mausoleum below the cathedral, the Embassy basement sat at garden level, and the dying sunlight filtered through windows, giving them just enough illumination to find their way through the cluttered space.

They reached a staircase that bent even farther downward, another level below the earth. Isabelle swallowed, her heart thudding in fear. "Do you seriously know where you're going?"

"Of course I do."

"Where?"

"The dungeon." He pulled her close beside him as he took the first step downward.

Isabelle followed, not so much because she trusted him but because she knew for certain, thanks to the comment of the soldier above them, that Valli wanted her captured. If Levi could prevent that from happening, she'd follow him anywhere, even into a dungeon.

"I just want you to know," she whispered, pulling instinctively closer to him as the filtered light faded to utter darkness, "that I have no intention of hiding in another crypt. That was the most terrifying thing that's happened to me since—" She broke off, thinking.

"Since the soldiers tried to take you to Valli?"

"That was afterward."

"You've had quite a day." He pulled out the small flashlight he'd taken from the soldiers. Its beam cut through the darkness, landing on ancient chains that dripped from the walls. Isabelle tried not to think about the prisoners who'd been shackled inside the dungeon over the years.

"So where are we going?" She couldn't hear any soldiers following them and so assumed it was okay to speak in a normal whisper. It made the darkness feel slightly less oppressive that way.

"Back into the catacombs. From there we can get just about anywhere."

"There's an entrance to the catacombs under the Embassy? Why didn't we come up this way earlier?"

Levi cleared his throat.

Was he buying time before answering? Isabelle wasn't sure, but she didn't like it. Why had he risked their flight across the street if they could have come up through the Embassy?

When Levi finally spoke, his words were less than encouraging. "There's not really an entrance to the catacombs under the Embassy. According to the hand-drawn maps I studied, there used to be one, but it was walled over to prevent the catacombs from being accidentally discovered by the Americans." He reached the back corner of the dungeon and stopped, his light shining against the formidable bricks of the cold stone wall.

Isabelle shuddered, acutely aware of the fix they'd gotten themselves into. The lines of mortar that ran between the stones were dark gray throughout most of the subterranean room, but in the space where Levi shined his light, the mortar looked paler. Fresher. "So what are we supposed to do? Dig our way out?"

"Hold this." Levi handed her the flashlight. "Stand back."

Isabelle obeyed, hoping that whatever Levi was going to do wouldn't take l ong. What if the soldiers looked behind the bushes and realized they'd come back in through the window? They'd catch up to them quickly if that was the case.

Levi ran his hands along the seams between the large stone bricks. A few grains of mortar crumbled out from between the seams, and he pulled a tool from his pocket, chiseling away at a seam between the stones. Mortar fell like dust. Several hacking motions later, Levi stood back, a satisfied look on his face.

"I need something big and heavy," he murmured, looking around.

"What for?"

"To use as a battering ram."

"You can't possibly expect to force your way through a stone wall."

"It's a false wall," Levi corrected her. "I could probably kick it in, but I don't want to risk an injury."

While he spoke, Isabelle looked around them at the deep underground prison. Like many of the buildings in the millennia-old city, the Embassy had been rebuilt and refurbished many times over the centuries, and discarded building materials cluttered the room. "Here's a beam," she offered, pointing with the flashlight Levi had handed her.

"Good work." Levi snatched it up, hefted the weight of it in his hands and balanced it on his shoulder. "Stand back."

Isabelle did so. She wasn't nearly as sure of Levi's plan as he seemed to be, and she feared that his efforts might bring the ceiling crumbling down on top of them or, at the very least, alert the soldiers to their presence.

The thick end of the old wood thudded against the stones as Levi pummeled it a few times. Then he appeared to brace himself, took several steps back and came at the wall at a run.

"Augh!" Levi exclaimed as the beam buried itself deep in the stones and he stumbled from the impact.

"Shh!" Isabelle hurried to his side. "Are you all right?"

The bodyguard looked stunned as he eased himself to his feet. "I'm fine," he said, though he didn't sound fine. He tugged at the beam and the stones shifted, crumbling away to reveal a round hole half a meter in diameter. The dust settled, exposing utter blackness beyond.

Isabelle shuddered. "Do you think the soldiers won't notice the hole and guess where we've gone?"

Levi pulled off his sunglasses as he turned to face her. His blue eyes were piercing in the silvery beam from the flashlight. "Your father's generals know about the catacombs," he stated bluntly. "They were there when your father shared the maps with me. If Lydian soldiers are answering to Valli, he must have at least one general under his thumb somehow. This tells him nothing he doesn't already know." He reached for her hand. "Would you like to go first?"

Although the hole hardly seemed large enough to squeeze through, Isabelle realized they didn't have time to enlarge it. And the fact that Valli likely knew about the catacombs made their flight that much more urgent.

Reluctantly, Isabelle placed her hand in Levi's and climbed over the pile of rubble to peer into the darkness of the hole. "You do recall that we left several soldiers in the mausoleum, don't you?"

"I'm sure they've left by now." Levi shined his flashlight into the darkness beyond. "It's less than a meter to the floor. We should hurry."

Realizing he was right, Isabelle hoisted the skirt of her evening gown just high enough to permit her to step through the hole. Her feet found the floor beyond and she secured decent footing among the jumbled stones. As soon as Levi was through she reached for the jacket he wore.

"I'm cold." Even her voice shivered.

Levi pulled off the tuxedo jacket and placed it around her shoulders. "I should have given it to you sooner. I don't need it." His white cotton shirt rose and fell against his muscular chest as he sucked in deep breaths, obviously still winded from the exertion of breaking through the wall.

Slipping her arms through the sleeves, Isabelle turned away from Levi and tried not to think about how indebted she was to the handsome bodyguard for all he'd done on her behalf that evening. Instead she focused on the path ahead.

Isabelle knew they didn't have much ground to cover because the Embassy was so close to the cathedral. They rounded a corner and found themselves back at the staircase that led up to the mausoleum. The climb that had been so frightening the first time now felt familiar, although Isabelle knew they had just as much to fear—possibly more so now that the soldiers knew she was alive. When they lifted the opening above, artificial light continued to shine down brightly from the central hall.

Levi paused. "Do you hear anything?" he asked after some silence.

"Nothing."

"Then let's go."

They clambered through the hole and darted down the hall. Isabelle saw no sign of the soldiers they'd left behind less than an hour before. Relieved that the men weren't still there, Isabelle nonetheless wondered where they might have gone. Her fingers tightened around Levi's arm, and her steps slowed.

"We need to hurry," he reminded her.

She shook her head. "Hurry where? You said yourself this is the last place they'd likely look for us. If we go running upstairs we could be captured."

The dark line of Levi's beard flexed as he clenched his jaw. He seemed to weigh her words carefully before he spoke. "The soldiers have already checked the cathedral—I have no doubt about that. They'll most likely assume we've fled the area. They'll widen the perimeter of their search area before they recheck where they've already been."

"Do you think so?"

His blue eyes hardened. "Whoever's behind this insurgent uprising, they seem to have gained control of the Lydian military. That means Lydian commanders following Lydian protocol."

Isabelle recalled his earlier insinuation that he'd served in the Lydian military. Although she wanted to question him about it, there simply wasn't time. She followed him down the hallway toward the steps that led up to the cathedral. "How long do you think we'll have before they circle back and check the cathedral again?"

"It depends on how organized they are. They've just pulled off a major ambush so I'd like to believe they won't be too methodical about their search just yet. We might have an hour, maybe several hours. We still need to move quickly."

"And where are we moving to? Do you still think you can get me out of the country?"

A smile twitched in the corner of Levi's eyes. "Now you want out of the country?"

He looked far too pleased with her change of priorities, but Isabelle refused to be distracted from her goal of reaching safety. "If Stephanos Valli is working with the insurgent forces, then yes, I want to get as far from here as I possibly can."

"Then we'll need help." Levi led her up the stairs to the back hallway of the cathedral, where the stone floors gave way to Persian rugs, softening their footfalls. "One of the deacons at the Cathedral is a former Sanctuary International agent. If he's here— if we can find him before anyone else recognizes you—perhaps he can help us get to out of the country. The Sanctuary International headquarters are in New York City. We'll be safest there."

Isabelle nodded. "What does this former agent look like?"

"I don't know," Levi admitted. "We've never met, but your father mentioned his name in passing—"

"What's his name, then?"

"Dan? Don? Dom?"

"Dom Procopio?"

"Yes." Levi snapped his fingers. "I think that's it."

"Dom Procopio is a deacon and a friend of my father," Isabelle offered cautiously. They'd made their way down the richly inlaid hall, and now the doors to the deacons' offices appeared in front of Isabelle as she turned the corner. The name *Dom Procopio* was etched into the placard on the third door, and Isabelle grasped the doorknob with her right hand.

Levi's calloused fingers covered hers. "Careful," he cautioned her, suddenly so close that she could feel his warmth still the goose bumps on her arm. "We don't know what we'll find on the other side of that door."

Isabelle swallowed but didn't dare turn around to meet his eyes. She'd spent too much time getting close to Levi already. Needing to put some space between them, she cautiously cracked the door open just far enough to allow her to see inside the room.

Dom Procopio sat bound to his desk chair, a thick gag stuffed into his mouth.

Isabelle wondered if he was even still alive.

FOUR

Levi hurried to Dom Procopio's side and pulled the gag from the former-agent's mouth. Relief filled him as the older man gasped for breath. The deacon's bulbous eyes rolled as he searched the room and widened when he spotted the princess.

"Your Majesty!" Dom looked as though he would have bowed if he hadn't been tied to the chair. "They said you were dead."

"Not as long as I have any say in the matter." Levi rushed to untie the stubborn knots that bound the man's hands behind his back.

"And who are you?"

When Levi introduced himself and explained that he was an agent with Sanctuary International, the deacon's face brightened immediately.

Isabelle joined Levi at Dom's side, her nimble fingers making quick work of the bindings at his ankles. "Who told you I was dead?"

"It was on the news," Dom gestured with his newly freed hand toward a small television set in the corner of the office. "I heard the explosions outside and tuned in to find out what was happening." He leapt up as soon as Isabelle had freed his feet and switched on the television. Images of smoking vehicles filled the screen. "See for yourself."

Though Levi didn't want Isabelle to have to relive the attack via the breaking news report, at the same time they both needed to know what was going on. He said a silent prayer that nothing on the screen would be too painful for her to see.

But the chaos surrounding the news broadcast provided little in the way of answers.

"All members of the royal family are at this time presumed dead," a solemn-faced reporter announced. Levi recognized the silver-haired man from the local Lydian television station. "Although no bodies have yet been identified, the royal motorcade was destroyed in the ambush, and there is no sign of any surviving member of the royal family."

Levi turned and looked at Isabelle, whose eyes were riveted to the screen. Her lower lip trembled slightly and she pulled his tuxedo jacket tighter around her shoulders.

"I'm sorry," he said, torn between pulling her into an embrace and maintaining an appropriate distance.

The scene on the television split, and half the screen showed an anchor in a newsroom. "Paul," she addressed the on-the-scene reporter, "we've heard rumors of possible sightings of members of the royal family since the blast. There was even a report that Princess Anastasia and a member of the Royal Guard were attacked at the marina. What do you make of these claims?"

"It's difficult to say at this time." Paul's solemn expression became more intent. "The attacks came out of the blue. The scene here on the street is one of disbelief and chaos. All we can say for certain is that none of the bodies have been identified as any member of the royal family."

"No bodies have yet been identified," Isabelle repeated, meeting his eyes. "But they're still assuming I'm dead. Maybe I'm not the only one who escaped." Hope glimmered behind her unshed tears.

Levi realized that Isabelle needed to remain optimistic that her family members might have survived. If she believed them to be dead, she might be immobilized by grief. "Maybe," he concurred. He wished the reporter could tell them who was behind the attacks, but as the footage looped back to the scenes they'd already witnessed, Levi realized it was likely that no one knew any more about what had happened.

He turned his attention back to Dom. "Who tied you up? Soldiers?"

The man's eyes bugged wide. "Lydian soldiers. They asked if I'd seen any members of the royal family. I was shocked because the television said they were all dead."

Isabelle's chin lifted defiantly. "At least one of them escaped."

A warm smile lit Dom Procopio's face. "At least one," he agreed. "And the soldiers didn't specify who they were looking for. Perhaps all of your family is at large."

Levi was grateful to the man for his encouraging words and for the insight he provided. His mind lit upon a detail he'd almost overlooked. "The soldiers we fought earlier in the mausoleum—one of them looked at me and said, 'Alec?'"

He met Isabelle's eyes and she regarded him solemnly for a moment. "Your blue eyes—my brother Alexander has blue eyes. And with your beard covering so much of your face, if the soldiers were looking for my brother, they might have thought you were Alec. He's served many years in the Lydian army. Most of the soldiers know him."

"So your brother may be unaccounted for," Levi concluded.

But Isabelle was clearly thinking about something else. "The soldier in the Embassy, the one who said Valli would be pleased that they'd captured me— he's a friend of my brother. Sergio Cana."

"Do you think Sergio said what he did to warn us?"

A hope-filled smile spread across Isabelle's lips.

"I believe that's exactly what he was doing. If he hadn't said what he did—if we'd have waited one more second to act—we might well be in Valli's hands right now."

Her words sent a chill up his spine. If they waited one more second to act, they might yet fall into Valli's hands. Levi closed his eyes for a moment and prayed, "Lord, may Sergio Cana not be punished for his bravery. And may we not waste his efforts." Then his eyelids snapped back open and he met Isabelle's eyes. "We need to get moving."

Dom Procopio rubbed his wrists where they'd been bound. "I will help you in any way I can. What is your plan?"

"We have to get the princess out of the country."

"That is wise," Dom agreed. "But judging from the number of soldiers who searched the cathedral earlier, I would guess that to be a very difficult task. Perhaps we should try to hide her inside the country."

"No." Isabelle inserted herself firmly in the discussion. "That would only give the insurgents greater opportunity to move forward with their plans. I *must* reestablish the rule of my family. I can't do that if I'm in hiding."

Levi placed a calming hand on her shoulder. "We'll get you out of this country." He turned to Dom. "We're less than two miles from the Sardis airport. Do you think you can get us there?"

"Get you to the airport?" Dom repeated, his round eyes thoughtful. "It might be possible, but you'd never get on a plane. Both of you would need passports, for one thing. And even if there were no soldiers at the airport, which would shock me, Her Highness is certain to be recognized."

The older man made many good points. Levi continued to brainstorm. "The coast is just as close. Could you get us to a marina?"

"Do you have a boat?" Dom asked.

Levi shook his head regretfully.

"We could go through the mountains," Isabelle suggested.

Levi felt a jolt of fear at her suggestion. "We'd have to travel across the whole country. That's more than a hundred kilometers."

"And it's the last place they'd think to look."

Dom took her side. "There's a Sanctuary outpost on the Albanian border. You could cross there."

The same outpost where the fated message had been delivered by a man who ended up dead? Levi shook his head. "I don't know—"

"We'd still need passports to cross at the border and to make an international flight from Albania." Isabelle sighed. "My passport is back at the palace."

Levi reached inside a pocket on his bulletproof vest. "I have you covered there, Your Majesty." He held out his own passport and the fake passport Sanctuary had supplied him for the princess, which used an assumed name. "*If* we could get to the border—"

"I can get you to the border," Dom interrupted. "And I can get you across into Albania, no passport necessary. You can save that for your flight. The princess is far less likely to be recognized by Albanians than Lydians."

Unsure what the deacon meant, Levi looked into his round eyes. "You can get us into Albania without passports? How?"

"The Mursia River."

"All the bridges have border-crossing checkpoints."

"You're not going to use a bridge." Dom's smile was unsettling.

Levi opened his mouth to protest, but Isabelle cut him off. She'd been looking over his shoulder at the fake passport he'd provided. "This is a most unflattering picture of me."

"It was doctored," Levi explained, "to make you look less like a princess. The idea was to make you uglier because it hardly seemed possible to make you any prettier."

If Isabelle recognized his compliment as such, she didn't acknowledge it. "I look depressed. And bloated."

Dom peered at the picture. "You look nothing like yourself and yet just enough like yourself to pass for yourself. Sanctuary did a good job on this. It just might work."

The princess beamed at him. "Let's do it then. We need to hurry. Those soldiers could return at any moment." She turned her royal smile on Dom. "How are you going to get us to the river?"

While Levi struggled to think of how to talk Dom and Isabelle out of their crazy plan, the former Sanctuary agent outlined his strategy.

"The Cathedral Charity Store has a delivery truck. We often take excess donations across the border to ship to needy people in Eastern Europe, so it won't look out of place. Right now the back of the truck is filled with bags of donated clothing. The princess can hide among the bags." Dom looked at Levi. "As long as no one is looking for you, I suppose you can ride in the front with me."

"They'll recognize him," Isabelle explained. "The two of us went into the Embassy earlier. The security cameras surely got plenty of footage. If he's associated with me, we can't risk letting anyone see him."

"Fine. He can ride in the back of the truck, too." Dom switched off the television and headed out the door. "Let's get moving."

Shaking his head inwardly, Levi hurried to keep up. He could already imagine how his father would criticize the flaws in their absurd plan if his mission failed. Silently, he prayed God would help them out of a situation he feared was doomed from the start.

Isabelle nestled among the large plastic bags of donated clothing and prayed her hiding place wouldn't be discovered. She'd been in worse spots before, not even including what she'd experienced already that evening. How many times had she traveled to Africa with mission groups building deep water wells in remote villages? How many hospitals and schools had she visited in those tiny towns— and via far more rustic conditions than a truck filled with bags of clothing? At least she was warm and the bags of clothes were soft, cushioning the bumpy ride in a truck whose shocks, she realized, were shot. She made a mental note to donate a new delivery truck to the Cathedral Charity Store.

Assuming she survived long enough to do so.

"Are you doing all right?" Levi's voice carried clearly through the enclosed rear of the truck, in spite of the piles of bags that separated them.

"So far so good." She sighed, realizing how the attack and her flight from Lydia would change her plans. "I was supposed to be getting ready for a mission trip after the state dinner. I had originally planned to leave earlier this week, but then I would have missed the dinner. Now three African villages are going to have to wait for their deep water wells. Innocent children will continue to be exposed to deadly diseases from filthy water supplies. Do you think the insurgents thought of that before their attack?"

"I'm sorry," Levi apologized, though Isabelle knew it wasn't his fault. "You do a great deal of mission work overseas, don't you?"

"I feel it's my duty as a person of privilege. I'm in a unique position to not only raise the funds to improve people's lives, but also draw public attention to the plight of those in need." Isabelle could picture the delighted faces of the children in the previous villages where she'd traveled to build wells. They'd been so jubilant when the water had started flowing. And the insurgent forces, by their rash act, had denied scores of children that happiness.

"I would like to promise you that we'll restore you to that position soon," Levi spoke with regret in his voice, "but I don't know what we're dealing with. Until we know who was behind today's attack, there will be little we can do to bring them to justice."

Isabelle sighed, the whole overwhelming situation more than she wanted to think about. Every time she considered the likelihood that her parents and siblings had died in the attack, she wanted to break down and cry. But there wasn't time to cry now. She had to focus on getting out alive. She owed that much to her family, whether they had lived or died, and to the children she hoped to someday help.

Trying to focus on the steps that would need to

be taken before she'd be safe in the United States, Isabelle said, "I'd like to change into something more practical when we get to the border. Surely somewhere in these bags there are clothes that will fit me." Isabelle had made many donations of her own clothing to the charity shop, though she doubted any of it would make the trip in the truck. It usually sold quickly and at a premium price that helped fund the cathedral's charity work.

"Good idea," Levi agreed. "We don't know who might still be looking for us, even when we get to Albania. We want to avoid drawing attention to ourselves."

"You're exactly right. That's why I think you should shave off your beard."

When her suggestion was met with silence, Isabelle explained, "If Valli is affiliated with the insurgents, and if the Embassy security cameras have your picture, you need to do everything possible to avoid looking like you did when we stepped into the Embassy."

"Good point." Levi sighed. "And we need a cover."

"Cover?"

"Yes. An identity. It's not enough to simply try *not* to look like a princess and her bodyguard. We've got to be someone else—someone far removed from who we really are."

Isabelle realized his point was a good one. Once they were out of the Balkan region, perhaps she could get away without being recognized as the Lydian princess, but there were too many curious people-watchers in the world who would wonder what kind of business they were on. "We could be traveling students."

"That would work. I'm a little old for that, though."

"How old are you?" Isabelle realized she had no idea, having not thought about his age before.

"Thirty-one."

"Hmm." Yes, she had to admit it was a little old for pretending to be a student. "We need to be something far removed from who we really are," she repeated his instructions, trying to prompt her brain to think of possibilities. "How about poor people? Because I'm rich in real life, we could pretend to be poor people. I would match my passport photo then."

"Poor people making an international flight?"

She grumbled in her throat. What then? She tried to think of the people she'd seen in airports the many times she'd flown back and forth to the United States when she'd gone to college there. People traveling on business…but then they'd have to think of some business to be affiliated with. Too complicated.

Levi's suggestion about being far from who they were stuck in her mind. "The media have a distinct impression of who I am," she admitted slowly.

"I know." Levi's words were soft.

Her heart squeezed with shame and anger at Stephanos Valli and Tyrone Spiteri for causing the situation that had created her reputation. "Ever since my failed engagement the media had labeled me as someone who's unloving. Cold."

"The Ice Princess." Levi spoke the title gently, but his words still pierced her.

"I'm not like that." She shoved back a tear that had sneaked out. "How many orphans have I held? How many impoverished people have I embraced? I'm not unloving."

"But you haven't been romantically linked with anyone. And Tyrone's words after you broke off the engagement—"

She couldn't let him speak the words out loud. "*He* is the one who fooled *me*. Our engagement was nothing but a scheme for more power. He didn't care about me." The memories welled up despite her attempts to squash them. "Tyrone saw me as just another possession. He wanted to take me to make himself feel more powerful."

"Did he—" Levi began but then stopped. "I'm sorry. It's none of my business."

But Isabelle felt the need to set the record straight. In the darkness of the back of the truck, with Levi far removed from her by bags of clothing, she felt safe enough to admit out loud what she'd never told the press. "He tried to rape me," she spat the words out. "When he realized I'd seen through his facade, he knew I wouldn't go through with the wedding so he tried to force himself on me." She straightened with the one shred of dignity she'd saved. "But I fought him off."

"Good for you," Levi sounded sincerely proud of her. "How—"

"When I was in the United States in college there was a self-defense demonstration on campus. They showed us an eye-jab maneuver. I didn't get it exactly right, but I injured Tyrone's right eye. He's nearly blind in it now—which I'm afraid only makes him hate me that much more."

"And that's why he maligned you to the media."

"Yes." Isabelle sighed. "He has them all convinced I'm too frigid to ever love a man. I suppose I could find a guy to have a fling with just to prove them all wrong, but that would be the wrong reason to start a relationship, and I won't do that to myself or some innocent man."

Levi was silent, and Isabelle wondered if she'd said too much. She hadn't talked about Tyrone in the two years since those events had taken place. She'd thought maybe she was getting over what had happened, but the vengeance she heard in her own words told her otherwise. Now she wished she hadn't spoken.

"Perhaps," Levi's voice carried quietly through the back of the truck, "we could use those impressions to our advantage."

It took Isabelle a moment to wrap her mind around what Levi was suggesting. "You mean, for our cover?"

"Yes. We could be a couple on a romantic get-away."

The moment Levi made his suggestion he feared he'd gone too far. Isabelle fell silent, and with regret he realized his idea likely only made her feel worse. He wasn't sure why she'd trusted him with the truth about what had happened to her. And now he'd betrayed that trust by proposing such a ridiculous idea.

"I don't—" she started, and Levi scrambled to think of some way to erase his suggestion.

But when she finished her sentence, he felt that much worse.

"I don't know how."

Levi's heart froze. "Your Majesty?"

"I'm sorry, Levi. It's a good idea. I just don't know if I could pull it off. I haven't ever really dated—I was quite sheltered for so many years. My parents were so protective of me I'd never really dated. Perhaps that's why I didn't realize sooner what Tyrone was after and all the things that weren't right about our engagement. I'm afraid I don't even know how a person ought to act."

Her confession tore at him. No wonder she'd let the media get away with calling her frigid. She didn't know *how* to prove them wrong, and she was far too sensitive a soul to flub up something so important.

"I shouldn't have suggested it," he apologized. "It sounded like a good fit, but obviously…" He cleared his throat, unsure when talking had become so difficult. "The student idea was a good one. Perhaps we should just go with that."

He heard her sniffle from the other side of the bags of clothes, and when she squeaked out, "Okay," he realized she was having difficulty maintaining her composure.

His hand stretched across the bags in the darkness, and he tentatively felt for her face. His fingers touched wetness, and he wiped away a stray tear before gently cupping her cheek in his hand. To his surprise, instead of pulling away, she leaned her head toward his touch.

If it hadn't been for the bags between them he might have pulled her into his arms. But then, he realized he ought to be grateful their circumstances prevented him from getting any closer to her. It would be so easy for him to forget that she was more than just a beautiful woman for whom he felt growing affection. He couldn't lose sight of the fact that she was royalty and likely the only surviving member of her family. He'd promised King Philip he'd protect his daughter.

And that meant keeping her safe from him, too.

With guilt, he wondered if he hadn't made the

suggestion of a romantic couple because of the growing affection he felt for her. Was he subconsciously trying to get closer to her? He had no right to feel the way he felt toward her. The sooner they could go their separate ways, the better off they'd both be.

Reluctantly he pulled his hand away from the warmth of her cheek. "It feels like the truck is slowing down. I wonder if we're nearing the border."

"The road has been curving quite a bit lately, which is typical of the mountain roads as we approach the border." Her voice held no more trace of emotion.

The truck eased around another corner and then slowed to a stop. Levi waited for Dom to open the rear door.

"If you'd like to find some clothes to change into, we can ask Dom if this is a good time."

"Okay."

A moment later the rear door of the truck cracked open and Dom's balding head was outlined by the moonlight. "We're at the Sanctuary outpost. I'm going to scope things out. You two stay out of sight for now." Then the door clicked shut and they were left in darkness again.

The minutes ticked by and soon Levi saw the greenish glow from Isabelle's phone.

"It's almost midnight," she whispered. "I hope Dom is okay."

"He's a professional," Levi reminded her, though he wondered how the aging man would fare if he encountered insurgents—and what the two of them would do if Dom ran into trouble.

A few moments later he heard the door to the cab of the truck open and the vehicle started again. His pulse kicked into high gear.

Isabelle whispered, "I hope that's Dom driving us."

"I hope so, too." The trucked rumbled over a bumpy stretch for what couldn't have been more than a few kilometers before coming to a stop again. In the stillness Levi could hear even footfalls as their driver came around to the back of the truck.

Levi reached for his sidearm and pulled it from its holster, aiming it at the door. Silently he turned off the safety and prayed.

FIVE

"Put down your gun, Levi," Dom said as he opened the rear door of the truck.

Relieved to hear the familiar voice, Levi engaged the safety and put his gun back in his holster. "How did you know I had my weapon drawn?"

"I'd be quite disappointed if you didn't. You're supposed to protect this little lady." Dom extended a hand to Isabelle as she waded over the bags in her evening gown. "Sorry for the excursion. Nothing appeared to be obviously amiss at the station, but I didn't recognize either of the men stationed there, and a still, small voice told me to get out of there. I've learned to listen when God talks to me."

"I appreciate that." Levi hopped out of the truck and looked back up the rutted path Dom had driven them down, which ran parallel to the Mursia River. He could just see the swirling waters beyond them in the moonlight. "Do you think anyone followed us?"

Dom blinked into the darkness. "If they did,

they're awfully good at avoiding detection." He shivered visibly. "But I don't have a very good feeling about this. We need to hurry."

"May I please change clothes first?" the princess asked.

Dom agreed that Isabelle should find some clothes among the bags in the truck. He made sure she had a flashlight and then closed the door for privacy. Then he walked toward the river with Levi and spoke in a low voice. "Levi Grenaldo." He looked him in the eye. "I knew your father. We served together in this area years ago. He's a good man."

"Thank you." Levi cringed just a little at the comparison. His father's shoes would be difficult to fill, but he was determined to do his best.

Dom continued. "Because I trusted him, I will trust you. I honestly don't know how you're going to get Isabelle to the United States, but I will give you the best head start I can."

The ominous assessment did little to bolster Levi's courage. "I appreciate that."

"On the other side of the river there is a woodpile. Hidden in the middle, under quite a bit of wood and a tarp, is a motorcycle."

"Has it been started recently?" Given the age of the man he was speaking to, Levi feared the bike might be reduced to a pile of rust.

"Every couple of weeks, at least, the owner of

the property on the other side gives the bike a go and makes sure it's filled with gas. But it belongs to Sanctuary, and I can't tell you how many refugees have traveled through this area on that bike."

"Where should I leave it when I'm done?"

"Park it at the airport. Someone will come along for it soon." Dom startled at a noise just downriver from them.

Levi spun around, pulling out his weapon.

"A raven." He lowered his gun as the bird took flight over the river.

"Ravens aren't active at night." Dom looked about warily. "Something startled that bird. You two had best get moving."

Levi rushed to the truck and knocked before opening the door. Isabelle had changed into a sloppy pair of oversize jeans with a bulky hooded sweatshirt. She looked less princesslike already. "We need to get moving."

"I can't find any shoes."

"Wear the ones you had on." Levi's sense of foreboding grew, and the hairs raised at the back of his neck as he listened to the vast darkness. "We need to hurry."

Isabelle slipped on the heeled leather pumps and clambered across the bags. She leaned toward him, and Levi caught her around the waist as she jumped down from the back of the truck. Too late he realized he wasn't prepared for such close contact with the princess. As she landed against him, she looked up and caught his eyes for just a moment.

His heart gave a lurch at the hopeful expression on her face. Did she really think he could get her to safety?

Could he?

She took a step back and he turned away. Too much still needed his attention. Joining Dom near the bank, Levi realized the older man held a crossbow.

"Perhaps you should shoot this." Dom held the heavy weapon toward Levi. "My eyesight isn't so good anymore, and you'll only get one chance to make a solid shot."

"What are you doing with that thing?" Isabelle asked as Levi took the cumbersome crossbow from Dom.

"There's a zip line attached to the bolt," Dom explained. "That's how you're going to get across the river."

Before Isabelle could react to Dom's explanation, Levi spun at the sound of rustling in nearby bushes.

All three of them looked in the direction of the sound. Levi could almost sense the presence of someone nearby, but in the darkness he could see no sign of anyone. The best he could do was hurry and get the princess across the river quickly. He'd hoped to change from his tuxedo before going any farther, but that issue seemed trivial compared to getting Isabelle safely out of Lydia.

"How does this work?" Levi looked over the bolt—the arrowlike projectile that would carry the zip line across the river. "Is there a pulley, or do we have to hold on with our bare hands?"

Dom reached across and touched a small steel bar. "It's a lightweight pulley. I'd recommend going one at a time. I'm not sure if it can hold you both." He pointed to a large tree across the river. "Try to sink the bolt solidly into that large tree."

Levi raised the crossbow and took aim. He didn't have much experience shooting crossbows, other than a brief orientation during his training with the Lydian military, but the tree was large and less than twenty meters away. And he had no other choice.

Just as he released the bolt a loud noise from behind startled him. He spun around, with no time to squint across the river in the darkness to determine if the bolt had hit his target. Two burly figures had jumped from the bushes along the riverside. One grabbed the princess from behind and appeared to be trying to carry her off, although her struggles hampered his efforts.

The second was locked in hand-to-hand combat with Dom. Levi hesitated only a second before slinging the zip line around the nearest tree branch and jamming the crossbow tight into the crook of the branch to secure it. Then he leapt at the man who was pulling the princess toward the bushes. Dom was a former agent. He would want Levi to attend to Isabelle's safety first.

Grabbing the muscular figure from behind, Levi attempted to wrench his thick arms away from Isabelle. He couldn't risk using his gun with the princess so entangled; instead he used two arms to pry away one of the hulking attacker's large fists.

Isabelle gasped and writhed but was no match for the strong figure who held her. Desperately trying to think of a way to free her, Levi recalled that Isabelle had fought off Tyrone Spiteri by jabbing at his eyes.

It was the only decent idea he could think of. Clambering higher on the man's back, Levi reached around the attacker's head and dug at his eyes. With a furious yell, the assailant let go of the princess and grabbed Levi by the arms instead, throwing him over his back.

Levi spun in the air, for the first time in many years grateful for the gymnastics lessons his mother had enrolled him in as a child. He landed on his feet and darted after the princess, who'd dashed toward the river the moment the burly man had let go of her.

His only hope to outrun their oversize assailant, Levi barely caught sight of Dom still exchanging blows with the other attacker as he sprinted toward the tree that held the zip line. Scooping Isabelle around the waist with one arm as he ran, Levi grabbed the pulley where it was attached to the crossbow he'd jammed through the joint of the tree branch.

To his relief, the pulley disengaged just as their assailant hurled himself toward them. Levi pushed off with his feet, and he and the princess zipped along the taut wire across the gurgling waters of the Mursia.

Despite the relatively warm June weather they'd been experiencing, Levi knew the river was fed by the melting snow of the mountain streams and would likely be frigid. "Pull your feet up," he whispered to the princess, doing the same.

Unsure if the bolt he'd shot across the river had made solid purchase in the tree on the far side, Levi said a silent prayer that the lightweight pulley would hold them and that the grip of the line wouldn't fail.

The pulley groaned in his hand as the bank appeared just beyond them. "Lord, please don't let us fall," Levi whispered, just as he wondered how they might possibly land without crashing into the tree. The moment they reached the bank Levi let go of Isabelle, hoping she'd drop onto the soft earth before he braced himself for impact with the tree.

But to his surprise, Isabelle clung to his shoulders, extending her legs as they flew toward the tree. He kicked out with his feet.

They had no more than slammed into the tree when he let go of the pulley, simultaneously twisting around and trying to fall backward so he wouldn't crush the princess.

They came down in a tangle. Apparently Isabelle hadn't anticipated that he would let go so quickly because she still clung to him as though for dear life, her face pressed against his shoulder as they fell.

"Are you all right?" Levi whispered, wanting to attend to the princess but at the same time aware of the urgent necessity of cutting loose the zip line. Though they'd taken the only pulley across, the men could still easily use the line to reach them.

Clearly stunned by the fall, she panted audibly before whispering, "I'm fine. We should find cover, though. I can't imagine those goons will let us get away that easily."

Relieved that she hadn't been injured, he looked across the river and saw the first of their burly attackers making his way hand-over-hand along the zip line. He was nearly halfway across the river—and the second man wasn't far behind.

"Cover yourself," Levi instructed Isabelle, stepping in front of her as he pulled out his gun and shot the spot where the bolt was embedded in the tree. Splinters of wood exploded from the tree, exposing most of the bolt. Levi shot the spot again, standing clear as the bolt snapped free of the tree. With sharp cries, both of their attackers plunged into the frigid river. A moment later, all Levi could see was swirling water.

Unable to spot any sign of Dom on the other side,

Levi risked calling out to him, "Are you all right, old friend?"

Dom's voice sounded weary. "A little worse for wear, but I'll be fine. The moment those two realized who was getting away, they lost interest in me."

"Glad to hear it! If you can get a message to the office in New York, let them know we're on our way. But be careful!"

"You're the ones who need to be careful." Dom's voice boomed back, stronger already. "Godspeed to you!"

"And to you!" Levi had spotted a wall of stacked split logs while he spoke to Dom. Pulling the princess up after him, he whispered, "This way!" and dashed toward where Dom had said the motorcycle could be found. He didn't know how many others might be right behind their two attackers. They'd have to move quickly.

Isabelle looked back at the Mursia River as Levi pulled her away from its banks. She tried to catch sight of the men who'd attacked them, but clouds had rolled in, obscuring even the pale light of the moon, and Isabelle could see nothing but the roiling waters. Had the men been swept downstream? Or were they even now crawling up the Albanian bank?

She turned her attention to Levi, who wrestled with something among the logs. "Can I help you?"

She tried to catch her breath from her fight with the huge guy who'd jumped her. Fear chased up her spine, but she shivered it away, reassuring herself that Levi had been there. He'd rescued her from that awful man and his breath-crushing grip. Perhaps she could trust Levi—as much as she could trust anyone.

"I've got it," Levi whispered, pulling back a tarp before tugging on something that looked like handlebars.

"Is that a motorcycle?" Isabelle asked, blinking at the chrome just visible in the darkness.

"Yes." Levi threw aside an armful of logs, freeing the rear tire. "This is our ride to the airport."

Isabelle had been wondering how they would make the 250-kilometer trip to Albania's only international airport, which was nearly a four-hour drive from the Lydian border. She felt inside the waistband of her jeans to where she'd tucked her satin clutch, which held her cash and her phone. She didn't dare use her phone—there was too great a likelihood that the insurgent forces might be able to trace any calls she made. The longer she could stay off the radar, the better.

And the motorcycle looked like it would do the trick. "Do we have helmets?" she asked.

"Two." Levi unearthed them once he'd freed the bike, tapping the helmets together to shake out debris from the woodpile. "Now let's get moving.

Those thugs who attacked us probably alerted others to our location before they jumped us. If they had confederates at the border station, they might cross into Albania and follow the highway looking for us—and that's the road we'll *have* to use to get to Tirana. Our only hope is to move faster than they do."

Nodding, Isabelle accepted the helmet and strapped it on. She didn't mind the idea of riding a motorcycle, but she sincerely wished she'd managed to secure more practical footwear. However, Levi was right. Their top priority was getting to the airport as quickly as possible. And maybe she would find a pair of boots or sneakers in one of the shops and boutiques inside the airport. She hadn't flown through the Albanian airport in a few years, but she recalled that it had enjoyable shopping.

Levi straddled the bike and patted the seat behind him.

With a gulp of courage, Isabelle hopped on the bike behind Levi. She had no more than tentatively wrapped her hands around his broad shoulders than he revved the engine and the bike moved forward.

They rumbled toward a rutted path in darkness.

"Perhaps you should turn on the headlight," she suggested.

"I don't want to give away our position."

"The engine noise does that." She found herself leaning close to his ear to be heard above its rumbling. "And we'll move faster if we can see where we're going."

"All right." Levi clicked on the light. "Pray this doesn't make us a target."

Isabelle pinched her eyes shut and prayed. The motorcycle picked up speed along the rutted road, and she could feel Levi shifting his weight from one side to the other to keep them from tipping on the uneven track. Hoping to help balance the bike, she focused on moving with him as he leaned to one side and then the other. The last thing they needed was to wipe out and injure themselves or damage the bike.

"Oh, Lord, get us out of here in one piece."

"What?" Levi's question made Isabelle realize she'd started praying out loud.

"Sorry. I was just praying."

"Well, keep it up. Here's the highway. Those guys' buddies could catch up to us anytime."

"Right." Isabelle peeked her eyes open just enough to see the paved track that wound its way up from the Mursia River through the mountains. Though she hated to think how easy they'd be to find on the highway, she knew of no other passable route through the jagged peaks. At least she'd gotten safely out of her own country. She could only hope the insurgents would move about less freely here.

With a smooth road stretching out before them, Levi picked up the bike's speed considerably. Isabelle relaxed now that she no longer had to worry about taking a spill on the rutted mountain path. She could feel exhaustion weighing on her, and realized she'd been up since six that morning. Though she wasn't about to attempt to pull out her phone to check the time, she knew it had to be well after midnight, and she was tired.

Gradually, as no one caught up to them and the road twisted endlessly before them, Isabelle's fears receded enough for her to contemplate the fix she was in. With her arms wrapped tight around Levi's shoulders and her body pressed to his, it was difficult not to think about the man who had done so much to secure her liberty.

She'd hadn't missed the compliment he'd paid her back in Dom's office—his comment that the Sanctuary agents had to make her picture uglier, since she couldn't be any prettier. Warmth spread through her at the memory of his kind words. Had he been trying to flirt with her? He didn't act flirtatious otherwise, but as she'd admitted to him already, she didn't have any experience with men. How would she know if he felt something for her? She felt her grip on his shoulders relax slightly as she pulled hesitantly **away** from him.

Levi **nudged** her with his elbow. "Don't fall asleep," he cautioned her. "I don't want you to fall off the bike."

Rather than let him believe she could possibly

nod off with danger so close on their trail, Isabelle held on more securely, tucking her head against his broad back, out of the wind. Levi was a good man. And maybe she wouldn't mind if he felt something for her.

After her experiences with Tyrone Spiteri, she hadn't wanted anything to do with romance. But as she held tight to Levi's strong shoulders and their motorcycle hurtled through the mountains, she realized for the first time that she might not be so against falling in love, if she could fall in love with someone like Levi.

Deep darkness had settled over the landscape. As they approached Tirana, Albania's capital city, Isabelle wondered if she didn't see a hint of light in the east, or if it was simply the light of the city ahead of them. Rinas International Airport was located just northwest of the city, and they were approaching from the south, so they'd have to skirt the western edge of the metro area to get there.

Several headlights pierced the sky behind them. "Can you tell if we're being followed?" she asked Levi.

"No idea. Too many people are traveling into the city. The sun will be rising soon. I'll do what I can to keep ahead of whoever might be following us, but I don't want to draw too much attention to ourselves, either. As long as we're not attacked, I'll be happy."

Isabelle settled back as Levi followed the signs

that pointed the way to the airport. When they arrived Levi found a place to park the bike, and Isabelle's legs wobbled unsteadily as she climbed off.

Immediately Levi's steady hand supported her back. He met her eyes. "You all right?"

"Just tired." She blinked back the sleep that had been creeping up on her all morning.

"You can sleep once we get on a plane. Until then, let's try to stick together." He discretely unbuckled a holster and gun, lifting the seat of the bike and depositing the weapon in the storage compartment. Isabelle realized it would do far more harm than good to attempt to bring the weapon inside, but she felt a twinge more vulnerable leaving it behind.

"Do me a favor." Levi reached toward her, plucking up the hood of her sweatshirt and settling it over her head. "Try to keep yourself covered as much as possible. I know this isn't your home country, but your picture is bound to have been on the news. Even if we've given the insurgents the slip, we can't risk anyone recognizing you. Not yet." He gently pulled the hood forward but didn't seem satisfied by what he'd accomplished. "Can you wear your hair down?"

"I never wear my hair down."

"Exactly. You're always pictured with it swept up. Even on your mission trips you wear it up in a ponytail." His hands rested on the pins that held her upswept hair in place.

"Good point. You'll have to help me."

With the rising sun threatening to shed light on their actions, Isabelle worked quickly to pluck the pins from her hair, letting the disheveled curls fall past the sides of her face.

"Now we'll try the hood." Levi pushed her hair forward as he settled the hoodie atop her messy mane. "How's that?"

"Itchy."

He made a face, then pulled out his sunglasses and perched the oversize shades on her nose. A smile crinkled the corners of his eyes. "There. You hardly look like a princess."

Isabelle couldn't help smiling with relief that he'd managed to disguise her identity somewhat. "Itchiness is a small price to pay in exchange for anonymity. Now let's get rid of your beard so no one recognizes me because of you."

They entered the airport and immediately the bright lights and early-morning stream of passengers made Isabelle feel slightly better. Levi found the ticket desk and used his own credit card to buy tickets for the next available flight to New York City via Rome.

She breathed a sigh of relief once that important step was completed and they'd made it through security to the departure area, where many of the shops were located. They still had a couple of hours before the flight would board. "Let's get rid of that beard." She gave Levi's scruffy chin a pointed look. "And I'd like to get some more practical footwear, if that's at all possible."

They found sneakers in her size and comfortable socks to go with them. When Levi once again used his credit card to pay, all Isabelle could do was pray the insurgents hadn't matched his name to the face on the Embassy security camera—and she promised to pay him back as soon as she had the chance.

After grabbing a bite to eat, they picked up a shaving kit, but Levi balked when Isabelle suggested he leave her alone while he went into the men's room to shave.

"I'm not letting you out of my sight."

"What are you going to do—shave in a drinking fountain? Besides, I'd like to use the ladies' room before we board our flight." She watched Levi's eyes narrow slightly—a move she'd already come to associate with him digging in his heels.

He led her to a large map of the airport on a brightly lit central kiosk.

"There." He pointed to a mark on the map. "Family rest room."

She rolled her eyes at the stubborn man. "We're not a family."

"No—" he linked his arm through hers and led her in the direction of the restroom "—but it only has one door, so no one can walk in on you and carry you off. I'll stand guard outside."

Because there didn't appear to be any families waiting to use the special restroom at the early hour, Isabelle relented to allowing Levi to stand guard outside while she went in. After freshening up and brushing out the last of her royal hairdo, she stepped out. "Now it's your turn. I'll stand guard."

"You're not going to stand alone out in the open." Levi tugged her back inside the restroom. "You can wait in here while I shave."

Uncomfortable as she may have felt sharing the small room with him, Isabelle knew Levi had a point. And because he promised not to do anything more personal than shave off his beard, she figured it wasn't too inappropriate. As he'd pointed out several times already, she had a royal duty to stay safe. If that meant standing by while Levi shaved, it was a small price to pay.

Unsure if she ought to be looking at him, Isabelle could identify little else in the tiny room to keep her attention and found herself watching Levi as the white shaving foam he'd bought was peeled back by the razor, leaving a trail of tanned skin behind.

"You're not used to wearing a beard, are you?"

"No. Our fathers agreed it would be best if I disguised my appearance somewhat because I was a member of the Lydian army for four years and we weren't sure who might recognize me—good or bad."

"Our fathers?" Isabelle repeated.

"My father worked with yours to coordinate my position filling in for Alfred."

Having accepted Levi's hasty explanation for his role in protecting her back when they'd navigated the catacombs, Isabelle now realized she understood precious little about how he'd been appointed. "Why did they select you to guard me?"

Levi focused his eyes on his reflection in the mirror as he shaved and moved his mouth little as he explained, "None of the royal guard could be trusted. We had no way of knowing who else might be in league with the insurgents. When King Philip called the Sanctuary office, my father recognized that whoever was sent to protect you would need some level of familiarity with Lydia. Because I had spent so much time in the country, I was the obvious choice." He tapped his razor against the sink.

Piecing together the bits of the story he'd shared with her, Isabelle clarified, "So you're usually a bodyguard in the United States?"

Finished shaving, Levi turned on the water. "I'm not usually a bodyguard. I work for Sanctuary as a lawyer." He bent his head over the sink and splashed water on his face.

Isabelle studied the smudged white tuxedo shirt that stretched across Levi's well-muscled back as he washed the last of the shaving foam from his face. His jacket had never made it across the river. She pulled a few paper towels from the dispenser and handed them to him as he turned off the water.

"You're a lawyer?" The revelation made her consider how close she'd come to being captured so many times—and she hadn't even had a real bodyguard to protect her. "That's the best Sanctuary had? They couldn't even send a real bodyguard?"

He lowered the paper towels from his face and his cold blue eyes met hers. For the first time she saw his whole face without the shaving foam and without the beard.

Oh, was he handsome!

Her heart gave a little flip as she saw—really saw—for the first time the man who'd saved her life so many times. With his face and neck bare of the dark hair, he suddenly seemed more human, and more vulnerable.

And, oh, was he mad!

He took a step closer to her in the tiny marble-tiled restroom. "I got you safely out of the country, didn't I? How many thugs have I wrestled in the past twelve hours? How many times have I carried you?"

Isabelle swallowed and tried to look away, but his eyes held hers. She couldn't answer his questions—she'd lost count already. And she couldn't think straight with the sudden realization that had hit her.

She didn't want Levi to be upset with her. If

they'd met under different circumstances, she could well imagine herself having a crush on him.

Maybe she had a crush on him anyway.

But it was far too late to make a good first impression. "I'm sorry." She reached for his arm, but he stepped back beyond her reach. She let her hand fall to her side. "You've been an excellent bodyguard. I was just surprised. And I'm tired."

He turned his back to her and pitched the shaving items into the trash. "I'm tired, too. I shouldn't have snapped at you."

Isabelle studied his face in the mirror. He'd been plenty good-looking with the beard, she realized, but looking at him without it made her weak in the knees. She reached out a tentative hand and wiped away a bit of foam by his ear.

"You had a little shaving cream," she explained.

He met her eyes, and she felt her heart melt a little bit more. She cleared her throat. "I trust you." She looked at the door and wondered what they'd face once they stepped beyond it. "You're the only person I trust right now."

Levi didn't smile. "I can only pray that I will not fail your trust." He stepped between her and the door. "Because I'm only a lawyer."

SIX

Levi stepped cautiously from the restroom with Isabelle at his side. He studied the face of each person who passed by them, wondering how long it would be before their pursuers caught up to them and how he could possibly recognize them when they did. He didn't doubt that they would eventually track them to the airport. His only hope was to be ready when the next attack came.

To his relief, no one accosted them while they waited for their flight, and they were able to board the plane safely. Levi mentally cataloged each person near them on the plane, alert for the possibility that any of them might be trailing the princess. But no one seemed to pay them any extra attention. And no one seemed to recognize the princess among them.

Granted, Isabelle didn't look particularly royal in her cast-off jeans and bulky hooded sweatshirt. Her hair still obscured much of the sides of her face, and the only traces of makeup that remained from the evening before were the dark smudges under her eyes. She looked weary.

"Try to get some rest," he suggested as she settled in to the window seat and he took the place between her and the aisle. "Even if the insurgents know we're on this plane, I doubt they'll make any move until we land."

"That's what I'm afraid of," she whispered, leaning close to his ear. "The men who were after us no doubt realize by now that we made it into Albania, and if they guess that we're going to fly out, this is the only international airport. Do you think they'll realize we might be headed to New York?"

"It *is* the logical place for you to go. Even if they don't realize the connection with Sanctuary, the United Nations is headquartered in New York City, and we may need their help getting the insurgents removed. They may have already guessed that's where we're headed."

"So they may be waiting for us there."

Levi had reached the same conclusion already but appreciated that Isabelle had grasped the situation. At least he didn't have to break the news to her. They weren't out of the woods yet.

Far from it.

He could only imagine the insurgents would become more desperate the farther Isabelle flew from their clutches. He was amazed the men at the river hadn't shot them on sight, but he wasn't about to mention that to the princess. She'd been through so much already.

Instead, he focused on easing her fears for their safety. "I'm the one they're least likely to recognize, especially now that I've shaved off my beard. We'll stay on the plane when it lands in Rome. I'll keep an eye out for trouble, but they may be waiting for us when we reach New York. When we exit the plane, I'd like you to stay close behind me. If possible, keep your face blocked from view."

"How am I going to do that?" As they whispered, Isabelle had pulled her face closer to his. Now he could feel her breath near his ear as she spoke and caught the sweet scent of the cinnamon roll she'd eaten at the airport.

Refusing to be distracted, he focused on the challenge ahead of them. "Keep your hair down and your hood up. That should help. Wear my sunglasses and walk close to me. Bury your face against my shoulder as much as you can."

"I thought we were going to try to act like students," Isabelle challenged him. "This sounds more like your other plan."

"For this purpose, acting like we're a couple may be more practical. Just hold my hand and try to keep your face out of sight." He dipped his head so he could see her eyes clearly and was surprised by how close their faces were in the tight quarters of the coach-class seats. His breath caught. "Can you handle that?"

Her warm brown eyes looked hesitant, but then a smile bent her lips. "It's too late to buy a burqa, so I guess your plan will have to work."

The smile warmed him far more than it should have, and he found himself smiling back. It occurred to him that he wouldn't have to fake anything to play a man in love with her. The real trick would be convincing himself that he felt nothing. "Good. Don't worry about our landing. Get some rest."

Their flight to Rome would last just over an hour—they wouldn't even change time zones—and Levi was determined to let Isabelle get as much sleep as possible. Although he was exhausted, he couldn't risk sleeping through their stop in Rome. Once they were back in the air again he'd rest on the flight to New York—assuming they made it that far.

To his relief, Isabelle slept through their stop, which was uneventful. Once the plane was in the air again, he settled in to rest. It was a ten-hour flight to New York, but with the six-hour difference in time zones, it would only be four hours later when they landed—just before noon if everything went smoothly. And Levi prayed everything would go smoothly.

* * *

Isabelle awoke somewhere over the Atlantic Ocean with a kink in her neck. Levi slept soundly with his head lolled back in his seat. She marveled that he could still look so handsome in such an awkward position.

A small plastic cup of liquid was perched on the tray front of her. Recognizing her in-flight Coke, she downed the drink, grateful for something to wet her throat after the dry air of the plane and hoping the caffeine would help her wake up.

The sunrise had caught up with them and now bright light streamed in through the cabin windows. Isabelle would have been surprised that Levi could sleep in the circumstances, except that she knew he had to be exhausted. She had been, too.

So much had happened since the last time she'd slept. The day of the state dinner had been a busy one, and she'd had just enough time to get ready and dash to her limousine before her entire world had been rocked by the blasts from the ambush. Her life now felt like the images she'd seen on Dom's television of the burned-out remnants of the royal motorcade: a smoking, hollow shell of what it once had been.

She thought back to that newscast and the absence of any bodies among the wreckage of the royal motorcade. Her father had been wise to keep her siblings separated. Was it possible her brother or sister had survived the attack? Isabelle recalled the way the hood of a vehicle had slammed into the windshield of her car. Could anyone have survived such a blast? Or might her brother have escaped before the explosion?

She could only be certain of one thing—she was alive. And as long as she was alive, for however long it took, she'd do what she could to bring the insurgent forces to justice. If any members of her family had lived long enough to escape, she prayed God would be with them and keep them safe.

As Isabelle's prayers for her family poured from her heart silently to God, the plane ride passed quickly. Soon she could see the Statue of Liberty welcoming them as she had many a weary traveler over the years. New York spread out beyond them as the plane neared JFK airport.

Because Levi looked so peaceful in his sleep, Isabelle was reluctant to wake him. When she finally nudged him awake as the plane prepared to land, she realized with regret that they didn't have much time to discuss where they were headed once they left the airport. She knew he planned to take her to Sanctuary International headquarters, but she had no idea where that was, other than being somewhere in the vast city.

As soon as his eyes popped open, Levi appeared to be in bodyguard mode again. "I'm going to call someone to pick us up," he explained quietly as he straightened from his slumped sleeping position. "But we'll have to be careful. We don't want to lead anyone back to the Sanctuary headquarters. The headquarters are disguised and unlisted. We can't risk giving away their location—for your safety and that of so many others. If I have any concerns that we're being followed, we'll take a circuitous route and switch cars if we have to."

"What if we become separated?" Isabelle had never had to navigate the city or its complicated transportation systems alone—and now was the worst possible time to have to learn.

Levi looked almost startled by her question. "You're going to stick so close beside me that no one can see your face," he reminded her.

"But if we have to switch cars—"

"Then go to the UN." He stood as the passengers rose to exit the plane.

Isabelle rose next to him and fluffed out her hair to hide as much of the sides of her face as possible before slipping on the sunglasses.

Then Levi wrapped his arm around her back and pulled her close against his shoulder. "Let's stay in the middle of the crush of exiting passengers. That will help obscure us. And you need to keep your head down. I'll keep an eye out for trouble."

Isabelle obediently ducked her head against his shoulder, pressing her cheek against the smooth cotton of his shirt. She could feel his pulse beating away with a steady, reassuring rhythm as they paused in line, waiting to leave the plane.

Her own pulse had kicked into an anxious staccato as she tried to anticipate what might be waiting for them. Much as she wanted to believe that they were almost to safety, she'd thought the same thing when they'd entered the Embassy in Sardis. And she'd been so very wrong then.

As they stepped into the airport the crowd shifted, and their fellow passengers dispersed. Although she'd flown into JFK more than once over the years, Isabelle hardly knew her way around the vast complex of gates. She kept her eyes on the floor and focused on matching Levi's stride as he made his way through the terminal, trusting him to find the way and avoid trouble.

The muscles in his shoulder tensed.

"What?" she whispered.

"I'm not sure—" he kept moving and didn't look down "—so many people are moving in the same direction, it's difficult to tell if any of them are following us."

Isabelle didn't know what to make of his comment, but she took it as a bad sign. She doubted Levi would have admitted his concern if he hadn't sincerely suspected someone was showing them undue interest. But there was little she could do other than keep her head down and keep moving.

She let herself breathe a small sigh of relief once Levi had completed his phone call to the Sanctuary office for a ride. "How are we doing?" she asked, keeping her face in his shadow as she looked up in an attempt to read his expression.

The slight smile on his lips was warm, but his eyes looked wary. "We're going to have to play the couple," he said, leaning down to nuzzle her forehead with his nose.

The contact surprised her, but she also found it comforting and had to remind herself that he was only acting. She leaned into him slightly. "You think we're being followed?"

His nose traced her hairline until his lips hovered just beyond her ear. "There are two men who've been behind us ever since we left the plane. One of them took your picture a moment ago, though I can't imagine he got much more than your hair."

Isabelle's breath caught and she rested her forehead against Levi, needing the comfort his presence offered, even if they weren't really the couple they wanted everyone else to see. As a member of the royal family, she'd had her picture snapped by strangers many times—but none of those strangers had been out to kill her.

"What are we going to do?" she asked quietly, aware that the man she spoke to wasn't a bodyguard or even a Sanctuary International agent. He was a lawyer, and for all she knew he didn't have any clue more than she did about evading the men who were after her.

But she didn't have anyone else to turn to.

"We'll have to kill time before the car arrives. I'm going to try to shake them. Whatever you do, stay close to me and keep your face out of sight. As long as they're not sure you're the person they're supposed to be following, we stand a chance of losing them."

Isabelle did exactly as she was told, keeping her face out of sight and hoping she and Levi looked like a romantic couple. They paused several times with Levi's arms around her, his face close to hers as they consulted about their next move, hoping to give anyone watching them the impression that they were two people in love, so absorbed with one another that they didn't care about anything beyond themselves. Their cover was so far from the truth— and yet Isabelle found herself wanting to believe it, to feel the affection Levi offered as he pressed his lips near her ear, to believe that the arms around her were not a shield, but a loving embrace.

"Now what?" Isabelle asked as they came to a stop near the doors to the outside.

"Here comes our car," Levi sounded hesitant, "right on time."

"Are we going to get in it?"

"Those two men are still watching us."

Isabelle's heart sunk. After all their maneuvering

she couldn't imagine the men were following them by accident. She wrapped both arms around Levi's shoulders, wishing there was some way she could hide. But obviously they'd already found her. She hiccupped back a fearful sob.

Levi's arms wrapped around her, pulling her closer into his warm embrace.

"Do something," she begged him, daring to look up into his eyes.

He bent his face closer to hers and his lips grazed the arch of one eyebrow.

Isabelle recalled all the negative articles that had followed her breakup with Tyrone Spiteri. They'd called her frigid, dispassionate, unloving. But she was none of those things.

Tentatively, she raised her face closer to his.

The men were searching for the Ice Princess. They didn't think she was capable of affection. Could she throw them off her trail?

Levi cupped her face in both hands, as though he could block all sight of her from the men who were watching. "Shall I?" he asked hesitantly, drawing closer by millimeters.

Instantly she realized what he was about to do. At the same second, she knew she sincerely wanted him to.

Unable to find her voice, Isabelle gave a tiny nod, and then Levi's lips met hers.

It was nothing like the kisses she'd shared with

Tyrone—*nothing* like them. Relief washed over her along with a rush of attraction toward the man who'd proved she really was capable of affection.

No matter what the media said.

Her hands tightened their grip on his shoulders and she rose up on her tiptoes as though doing so would help her kiss him better. To her delight, he didn't pull away but seemed to lose himself in the contact between them.

Lightheaded, Isabelle pulled back just long enough to catch a breath.

"They've turned away." Levi's words jolted her back to reality. "Now." He slipped one hand into hers and tugged her toward the car.

They were moving away from the station by the time Isabelle collected her thoughts. "Did they follow us?" she asked, still trying to straighten her head out after that mind-blowing encounter.

"No. I saw them looking back inside the airport as we pulled away—they're well out of sight now." He pulled back from her for the first time since they'd left the plane. "You can stop hiding for now."

"Thank you." She turned away from him and watched New York slipping by out the window. It would be wise, she knew, to keep her distance from Levi as much as possible. His kiss had only been meant to throw off her pursuers. In her head she knew that. Now if only she could convince her heart, which was leaping about inside her and couldn't seem to understand why she was no longer in his arms.

Meanwhile, Levi was on his phone talking in low tones and consulting with their driver. She quickly determined there was no point trying to sort out what was going on by listening to his half of the conversation. She'd leave that to him while she sorted through the crashing waves of emotion that assaulted her heart.

Levi's tug on her hand a little later pulled her out of her thoughts.

"Are we there?"

"No." Levi cleared his throat. "We're at Central Park. We're going to hop out and walk a few blocks while the car circles back again. If we decide the coast is clear, we'll get back in the car."

Isabelle didn't have to ask if he thought they were being followed again. She doubted he'd risk taking her out in the open if he didn't feel it was necessary. "And what if the coast isn't clear?"

"It's a big park."

"Levi?"

"We'll try to hide. I've got my phone. If I need to, I can ask Sanctuary to send out decoy princesses, but I don't want it to come to that."

"Why not?"

"Right now there's still a chance they aren't sure they're following the right person. If we send out decoys, they'll know you're in the city." He reached for the door handle. "Ready?"

"I guess."

They stepped out of the car and Levi pulled her into his arms again as they stepped onto the sidewalk. "As a precautionary measure, you should probably still keep your face out of sight. We don't need anyone recognizing you—no matter who they are. By now I'm sure the international news has reported the attack on your family. People everywhere will have seen your picture on their televisions. If they see you walking around their city, there's bound to be a fuss."

"We don't need a fuss," Isabelle agreed, keeping her face turned toward his shoulder, although his closeness was too fresh a reminder of the fantastic kiss they'd shared. But she was determined to follow his instructions until they'd reached safety. Then she could worry about keeping her distance from him.

Levi set a leisurely pace, stopping now and then to pull her into his arms, though she knew he was looking past her, not looking at her. She feared at any moment someone would leap out from behind a tree, but after some time, Levi surprised her by saying, "Here comes the car again."

"Is the coast clear?"

"I guess we'll find out." He tugged her back to the vehicle and they slipped quickly inside.

They drove around for a few more minutes before

Levi leaned back from conversing with their driver. "This may be our best chance." He scooped up her hand and met her eyes.

"Chance?"

"We're getting out a few blocks from headquarters. I don't want to risk leading them there, but I think—" he cast a glance through the back window "—I think we'll be okay." He opened the door and they stepped out onto a bustling sidewalk.

With her face turned toward Levi and her eyes on her feet, Isabelle wasn't even sure which part of the city they were walking through, but she stuck close to Levi and trusted him to get her to Sanctuary. As they crossed one street and then another, her hopes rose that they were going to make it to safety after all.

When they turned down an alley, Isabelle wanted to ask Levi where he was headed, but he quickly picked up his pace and, a moment later, broke into a run.

As Isabelle ran beside him she felt even more grateful that she'd been able to buy a pair of sneakers. She could hear footsteps pounding the pavement behind them. They had to get away! She tried to sprint faster. Seconds later a large figure jumped Levi from behind and he went down.

Thick arms wrapped around her, lifting her off her feet. She caught a glimpse of Levi struggling with two attackers as the thug who held her spun her around, carrying her quickly back up the alley the way they'd come.

Whipping her arm back, Isabelle managed to catch the brute in the nose with a hard jab from her elbow. His steps faltered as blood poured from his nostrils, but he kept moving.

Kicking at his legs as he carried her, Isabelle attempted to knock the man's feet out from under him. She could see a car running up ahead, parked at the entrance to the alleyway, its windows tinted just dark enough that she couldn't make out who waited inside.

She couldn't let the man get her inside that car!

Jabbing her feet toward his legs with desperate strength, Isabelle finally caught the man square on one knee. The joint buckled and he sagged toward the ground. She whipped back with her elbow again, this time catching him full in the face and sending his head snapping back with a grunt.

His grip loosened slightly and she flung herself from his arms, spinning around and tearing back down the alley toward where Levi was fighting off two other large men. With her loose hair streaming past her eyes she couldn't see much, but she ran toward him with everything in her, hoping to jump the attacker nearest her as soon as she reached him.

Footsteps tore up the alley behind her. She was nearly to Levi when a fresh set of arms plucked her up. She could immediately tell the man who held her was smaller than the one who'd carried her off the first time. He must have come from the waiting car.

Isabelle tried the elbow trick again but the man ducked, avoiding the blow. She extended her arm and managed to free her hand from his grasp. This smaller guy wasn't able to carry her nearly as swiftly as the first thug.

Swinging toward his face with her free hand, Isabelle managed to knock him in the ear. It must have stunned him because his progress up the alley wavered. She tried the move again and he lost more speed. Pulling back her arm for another blow, she hoped to free herself from his grasp in another moment.

She hardly heard the footsteps rushing up behind her until the moment before she felt the other man leap upon them.

SEVEN

Levi's head swam from the blows he'd taken, but he couldn't let that slow him down. He launched himself at the man who struggled with the princess, peeling him away from her just enough to allow him to get in a good slug at the attacker's jaw.

The man wavered in midair a moment. Levi caught him with an uppercut punch under the ribs and he seemed to deflate backward. Spinning around to face Isabelle, Levi was horrified to see her covered in blood. "Are you all right?"

She opened her mouth as though to respond, but at that very moment a large figure staggered toward them, bleeding profusely from his nose. The lumbering brute was enormous. Levi fought back the darkness that seemed intent on invading his line of sight. His struggle with the other men had left him on the verge of passing out. But he knew that if he lost consciousness, Isabelle would undoubtedly be captured.

Mustering what strength he had left, Levi thrust

his leg out in a high round kick and caught the thug near his ear. The man shook off the blow and reared toward him. Levi scuttled backward, wishing he had some weapon to use. Instead the best he could do was evade the oncoming attack.

The man came at him swinging and Levi ducked, avoiding the first blow but taking the second in a grazing shot along his jaw. Light exploded behind his eyes, but Levi blinked it back, shuffling out of the way as the man lunged at him again. He was aware of the princess just behind him.

"Run!" he told her, hoping this last attacker was the only one who remained.

"I don't know where—" she began to protest.

But Levi shook his head as he ducked away from another swinging fist. He held out his arms and continued backward, trying to block the bleeding man from reaching Isabelle. "Just get away. Anywhere."

The swinging fists picked up speed. Levi ducked back again and again before the attacker caught him in a solid punch to his gut.

Air whooshed from his lungs and the sky spun.

He heard Isabelle scream, and as he blinked back the blood that ran from a cut on his eyebrow, he saw the princess swinging something at their attacker's head. When he saw the man go down, Levi sagged forward in relief.

Isabelle stepped under his arm, and he slumped against her. "Stay with me, Levi," she whispered, patting his cheek. "Tell me how to get to Sanctuary before any more of those guys show up."

Stars danced behind his eyes, and Levi knew he was leaning heavily on the princess, but it was all he could do to stay conscious. When he spoke, his lips felt swollen and unfamiliar, and he realized the men who'd assaulted them had gotten in several hard blows to his face. "Down this alley. Two blocks. Don't let them—" he gulped a steadying breath "—see where we go."

"All right." Isabelle hoisted him a little higher and tucked one arm more securely around his waist. "Can you walk at all?"

Levi was able to get his legs moving, but the action seemed to demand as much from his system as he could possibly handle. After several steps blackness and stars clouded his vision, and he paused. "I'm sorry," he panted between breaths.

"It's all right."

"No." He wanted to look behind them to see if any of their attackers had roused, but turning his head only brought on another onslaught of stars, and his field of vision blurred completely. "Can you see the men behind us?"

Isabelle looked back for him. "They haven't moved."

Relieved to hear it, Levi nonetheless knew the men could regain consciousness and come after them at any moment. He couldn't let the princess be captured. Pressing on, he told Isabelle, "We'll come to a door on the right side of the alley that says *Sanctuary* in small blue letters. It's in the middle of the block. The pass code is eleven, sixteen, seventeen." His words came out between gulping breaths. "If the men come after us, drop me and run for that door."

"I'm not going to leave you," Isabelle protested.

Levi stopped on his tracks. He had to make her understand. "You will leave me," he said, fixing his eyes on hers. "It is your royal duty. You cannot endanger yourself for me. If those men capture you, I fear the Royal House of Lydia will end."

Isabelle absorbed his message with a solemn expression. Then she glanced back. "They still haven't budged. Come on. If we hurry, getting captured won't be an issue."

She propped him up a little straighter and moved forward, faster this time.

When his steps slowed, she all but pulled him. "Lean on me, Levi," she whispered. "We're getting there."

His closed his eyes and focused on matching her steps. When he faltered, she encouraged him, "Half a block more. I'll drag you if I have to."

The sky seemed to tilt and sway, and the next thing he knew, she had him propped against the doorway as she entered the numbers he'd given her. It seemed to take all his strength to make the step over the threshold. As the darkness closed in, he forced himself to fall forward so that he wouldn't block Isabelle from closing the door securely behind him.

Isabelle daubed gently at the wounds on Levi's face. She was certain the cut on his eyebrow could use stitches, but after the men who'd helped her carry him to the couch had found a first aid kit for her, they'd apologized about not being able to help more. There was a crisis somewhere, and everyone in the Sanctuary office was upstairs trying to resolve the issue. It occurred to Isabelle after the men left that *she* might be the very issue everyone was trying to resolve, but by the time that thought occurred to her, the men were gone.

She and Levi were on their own.

At least she was able to clean Levi's wounds and wash the blood from her hair in the nearby kitchenette. It saddened her, what those horrible thugs had done to Levi, leaving his handsome face swollen and bruised. After she'd bandaged up the worst of his injuries, she cupped his cheek in her hand, surveying the damage and trying to determine what else she might be able to do to help him.

After all, he'd done so much to help her.

Moments later, she felt his head shift in her hand, and Levi showed signs of rousing.

She couldn't help smiling down at him as his eyelids fluttered open. "I was afraid I was going to have to take you to a hospital," she chided him.

"Where are we?" He blinked several times.

"The back lobby of Sanctuary. At least I think that's where we are. Anyway, I entered those numbers at the door you told me to find, and it opened."

Levi's eyes seemed to come into focus. "Yes, this is the back lobby. You did an excellent job getting me here."

"I wouldn't have made it much farther." She closed up the first aid kit and gathered up the empty packets of ointment. Because he'd finally awakened, she wanted to keep him talking to help him stay conscious. "What were the numbers anyway?" she asked as she headed to a nearby wastebasket.

"Hmm?"

"The pass code for the door. Is that a Bible verse?"

"Ah." Recognition filtered across his face. "Ezekiel 11:16 and 17. 'The Lord says: Although I sent them far away among the nations and scattered them among the countries, yet for a little while I have been a sanctuary for them in the countries where they have gone. I will gather you from the nations and bring you back from the countries where you have been scattered, and I will give you back the land again.'" As he quoted the verses, his voice strengthened.

Isabelle felt a chill chase up her spine as Levi spoke the ancient words. "'I will bring you back.'"

She repeated God's promise softly, kneeling on the floor beside the couch where he rested. "'I will give you the land again.'"

"Those verses are part of the Mission Statement of Sanctuary International." Levi turned his head slowly toward her. "God was a sanctuary for the children of Israel. And we try to help people find sanctuary today, with the hope that someday some of them might be able to return to their homeland."

"I'd like to return to Lydia." Isabelle cleared her throat. "I'd like Lydia to be returned to my family."

As she spoke, voices echoed down the hall, and moments later several figures entered the room. One of the men who'd helped her get Levi to the couch led the way, explaining, "I didn't think to ask who they were. How was I supposed to recognize them covered in blood?"

As he spoke, a handful of men surrounded them, and a silver-haired man extended his hand. "Princess Isabelle?" he asked.

"Yes." She rose and shook his hand, warmed by his use of her title, in spite of her fear that it might no longer apply if the insurgents had taken over her government.

"I'm Nicolas Grenaldo, president of Sanctuary International. On behalf of our organization I'd like to welcome you and thank you for rescuing my son." He looked down at where Levi lay on the sofa. "He was supposed to be rescuing you."

Isabelle looked quickly back and forth between father and son, putting together the missing pieces. Levi hadn't told her that his father was the *president* of Sanctuary International. Even as she absorbed that news, she hurried to set the record straight. "Thank you for your kind words of welcome. I'm afraid I did very little to get us here. Levi fought off many assailants and carried me more times than I can count. We were nearly overcome in the alley when I was lucky enough to find a length of steel pipe to knock out the man who tried to kidnap me. Other than that little bit of effort, all the credit goes to your son that I'm alive at all."

Through the weary lines that had engraved themselves on his face, Nicolas Grenaldo beamed at her. "Praise the Lord for that length of steel pipe then and for your escape from those who would have harmed you. Our office has been turned upside down by the events of the past day, and we're making every effort to determine the fate of the rest of your family."

At his mention of her missing family members, Isabelle felt her heart catch, and her hands began to tremble. "Please, sir, do you know what has become of them?" She braced herself for the news. She'd been resigning herself to a grim outcome ever since she'd seen the first fiery blast sear the sky, but now she felt as though the gavel hung suspended in the air, ready to drop.

Sympathy filled the man's face, and Isabelle feared for the worst.

"You are the first member of the royal family to be recovered. We have no evidence to support the insurgent claims that your entire family is dead. There have been no bodies identified as members of the royal family. Our agents in Lydia have confirmed that none of those killed in the attacks fit the description of any member of the royal family. Indeed, the three dead have all passed preliminary identification. They were two drivers and a guard."

"Three bodies?" Isabelle heard her voice speaking, but she felt as though she was watching the conversation from somewhere else. No doubt, even if they weren't her family members, the drivers and guard would have been people she'd known. She grieved that they'd died so needlessly.

The man who'd stood by Nicolas's side now spoke up. "We believe that if the insurgent forces had any proof any member of the royal family had been killed, they would have made that news public knowledge. Moreover, they would have touted that as evidence of their victory. They have nothing to gain from hiding that fact, if it were true, and everything to lose."

"So my family may still be alive?"

Nicolas Grenaldo placed his hand on her shoulder. "We pray they are alive. More than that, we pray for their safety. You have overcome many obstacles in your efforts to reach us. The fact that the other members of your family have not yet made public the news of their survival means they likely are in no position to make their whereabouts known."

Isabelle struggled to untangle the meaning of his words from the decorum with which he'd spoken. "They're in danger," she realized aloud. "Likely greater danger than we have already faced."

Nicolas nodded solemnly. "We must continue to pursue every avenue for their rescue. But now, I must report the good news of your survival—"

Before the Sanctuary president could continue, Levi sat up straighter and interrupted him. "No. Don't let anyone know she's alive."

"What?" Father stared down at son in disbelief.

The act of sitting up must have been nearly too much for Levi because he wavered unsteadily before speaking. "We believe the American ambassador to Lydia, Stephanos Valli, may be in league with the insurgents."

Nicolas's face clouded. "That would be most unfortunate. We've been freely sharing information with his office."

"Stop sharing," Levi ordered, his tone much stronger now. "We cannot risk giving away anything. Not yet. Not until we know we can keep Her Majesty safe."

Isabelle felt grateful for Levi's defense. She didn't

want Stephanos Valli to know where she was—even if he already knew she was alive.

As she watched, Nicolas Grenaldo narrowed his eyes, and his balding head turned red. She could tell he was upset—whether with Levi or Stephanos, she wasn't sure. But his expression was forcibly pleasant when he turned to her.

"I'm sure you'll want to freshen up, Your Majesty. Levi will need to update our team. Samantha can take care of your needs now." Nicolas stepped back, and a youngish blonde woman led Isabelle down the hall.

"Right this way."

Levi watched Samantha Klein lead Isabelle down the hall, and his gut churned. Samantha didn't like him—not since he'd rejected her advances toward him a couple of years before. What if she conveyed her distaste for him to Isabelle? His father had already displayed a marked lack of esteem for his skills. What would Isabelle think of him?

He tried to convince himself it didn't matter what Isabelle thought about him—that he had played his role in her rescue and might never even see her again. But his heart refused to believe it.

"Levi—" his father turned and led the men away, calling back to him as he left "—clean up and meet me in the third floor conference room in twenty minutes. I need your intel, and I need it yesterday."

"I'll be right there." Levi stood on shaking legs and tried not to pass out. He had a bathroom with a shower off his office and a selection of clothes there. Other than his old room at his parents' house, it was the closest thing to a home he had. It was all the home he'd needed since he'd finished law school and spent all his time working.

He slumped against the railing in the elevator and made it to his office without passing out. Catching a glimpse of his reflection in the mirror, he cringed. His face was a patchwork of cuts and bruises, and blood continued to seep from the butterfly bandage Isabelle had stuck to his eyebrow.

Turning away from the mirror, he cleaned off and changed clothes. Despite of his best efforts, he arrived at the conference room twenty-three minutes after his father had left him. He was three minutes late—a fact his father would undoubtedly take note of and not forget.

"We've pulled up the file on Stephanos Valli." Nicolas shot Levi a look as he entered, communicating with certainty that he was aware of every second they'd waited. "He was born Steven Valli in Elmhurst, Pennsylvania, in 1953. His maternal grandfather had immigrated to the United States from Lydia, and his grandmother was of Greek descent. A perfect fit for the Lydian ambassador, between his Ivy League education and his pedigree. He even changed his name to Stephanos when he was appointed ambassador to Lydia to make himself more relatable to the Lydian people. So what makes you think he's in league with the insurgents? What would he possibly have to gain when he clearly would have so much to lose?"

"I tried to take Isabelle to Valli after the ambush." Levi placed both hands on the conference table, as much to prop himself upright as to make eye contact with his father across the table. He realized much of his negative impression of Valli was based on Isabelle's repugnance toward the man. But they had facts on their side, too. "When we entered the Embassy there were Lydian soldiers standing guard. Two of them tried to take our weapons. A third, whom the princess identified as being a friend of her brother, Alexander, made a statement that Isabelle felt was intended to warn us away from Valli."

"What did the soldier say?"

Levi did his best to quote the man verbatim. "He said, 'Oh good, you've captured the princess. Valli will be so pleased.'"

"Captured?" Nicolas Grenaldo breathed the word with incredulity in his tone. "Why would Valli want to capture the princess?"

"Why would anyone want to destroy the royal family?" Levi met his father's eyes. "The nation of Lydia is a small, peaceable country with little economic impact and no known enemies. What would anyone have to gain?"

The sound of a throat clearing behind him sent Levi spinning around.

Isabelle entered the room. She wore khaki slacks and a simple navy button-down blouse, and her still-damp hair hung in drying curls down her back.

The sight of her took Levi's breath away. "Your Majesty." His throat was suddenly dry.

The princess must have heard the last of their conversation because she jumped right in. "Stephanos Valli has tried to manipulate my family for his own benefit before. He convinced my father to initiate a marriage contract between me and Greek businessman Tyrone Spiteri. When that agreement ended, Valli made it very clear where his allegiances lay."

Nicolas nodded. "Valli criticized the royal family for ending the engagement."

"Yes." A touch of color rose to Isabelle's cheeks. "He publically maligned me and tried to undermine the authority of my father's rule. Were it not for my father's affection for the United States and his connection to this country through my mother, he would have had Valli removed from Lydia."

The Sanctuary president absorbed the information. "We don't know why the royal family was ambushed. No one has stepped forward to claim responsibility for the attacks. It's possible Valli might be involved." His silvery eyes roved the room. "But you said *Lydian* soldiers were guarding the Embassy. The king is the head of the army. Who told them to capture the princess?"

Isabelle shook her head thoughtfully. "Three generals serve under my father. I am on familiar terms with David Bardici, Corban Lucca and Marc Petrela. I hate to think they would conspire against the royal family."

"I hate to think anyone would do this," Nicolas Grenaldo commiserated, "but someone did, and your generals have done nothing to stop it. Corban Lucca was in the motorcade at the time of the ambush. He has not been heard from since. We've been in contact with Bardici and Petrela, but neither of them have said anything to indicate any animosity toward the crown or involvement with the insurgents."

"Someone has to be working with Valli." Levi wouldn't let them lose sight of the facts. "Host country officials are not allowed to enter a representing country's embassy without permission. Yet those Lydian soldiers appeared to be stationed there and answering to Valli. That tells us there is a conspiracy at work here, and Valli *must* be in on it."

Isabelle nodded her agreement. "What about the prime minister? Have you been in contact with Gloria Emini?"

"Prime Minister Emini has Parliament at the ready to host a special session as soon as need arises, but she cannot hold an official session without the consent of the ruling sovereign." Nicolas gave Isabelle a pointed look. "Her biggest concern is locating the Head of State or, in the king's absence, crowning a successor."

Isabelle's face blanched noticeably.

Levi understood what his father was getting at, and no doubt Isabelle did, as well. But for the sake of everyone else in the room, he noted, "Once the crown has passed from King Philip, he will have no further legal claim to the throne. He cannot reclaim the crown."

"My father and mother had four children." Isabelle's voice filled with emotion as she spoke. "My oldest brother, Thaddeus, who should have been the heir, disappeared six years ago and was presumed murdered. My brother Alexander is the second child and heir apparent. I am next in line to the throne following Alexander, and my sister, Anastasia, is after me."

Nicolas Grenaldo's deep voice carried clearly in spite of the gentle tone he used. "Regardless of who may technically come before you, Isabelle, you are the only one we know to have escaped the attack. You are the only person who can reclaim the crown on behalf of the royal house of Lydia."

"I can't." Isabelle shook her head. "I can't claim the crown, not while there's still a possibility that my father may be alive."

"You may not have a choice," Nicolas said firmly.

"I may not have the option," Isabelle protested. "I fled the country to save my life. Is it safe for me to return?"

"We can make it safe."

"How?" Levi demanded his father explain. "We don't even know what we're up against. We don't know who our enemies are."

"Perhaps we need to flush them out," Isabelle murmured, almost to herself.

"What about the UN?" Samantha Klein asked, stepping out from behind Isabelle's shadow. "Can't they protect Isabelle? Why haven't they done anything to intervene?"

Levi barely had to raise his head to answer. "Did the UN intervene when John F. Kennedy was assassinated? Did the UN step in when the President of Poland and dozens of other Polish leaders were killed in a plane crash? No. Because their governments had rules of succession in place for just such an eventuality. What is the current situation in Lydia?" Levi addressed his father. "Is the military having any trouble keeping the peace?"

Nicolas looked solemn. "Other than the piles of flowers being placed at the gates of the royal palace, little has changed. The military is keeping the peace. Government bodies—the postal service, police, airport authority—are all operating on faith that the situation will be peaceably resolved. But how long they can remain operating in a state of anarchy is anybody's guess."

"I don't believe there is a state of anarchy. Someone is calling the shots," Isabelle insisted. "Someone has committed a crime against my family—and they're still committing it as long as they remain at large."

"We don't know who," Nicolas acknowledged. "Perhaps we should send in a team to investigate Valli, to find out who he's working with and who is behind the attacks." He looked around the room.

The men who had been standing silent for so long now looked down and away. Their response didn't bother Levi. Without Lydian connections he couldn't imagine any of them making inroads—certainly not as quickly as they needed them made. Levi supported his father's plan. "If we can bring evidence before the UN Security Council that an act of aggression has been committed, that the current situation presents a threat to the peace, then the United Nations could be compelled to intervene. All we need is proof. We need someone on the inside. Someone who can get an audience with Valli and the generals."

"I'll go." Princess Isabelle spoke without the slightest hint of hesitation in her voice.

Levi opened his mouth to protest. Only the day before she'd trembled with fear at the thought of facing Valli again. "Isa—"

"My family may be alive somewhere." She cut him off before he could say her name. "If they are, I have no doubt they face grave danger. Every minute the insurgents remain in power increases the odds that my family members may be captured or killed. The only thing I can do to help them is to learn who was behind the attacks and bring that party to justice. We must act quickly. The lives of my parents and siblings are hanging in the balance."

Levi watched the princess with pride and growing affection. He knew her fear of Valli was strong, but love for her family was stronger.

Nicolas Grenaldo nodded solemnly. "You will not go alone. We can assemble a team to provide backup for you. And I will send my son as your coagent."

"Levi and I have learned to work well together."

"I'm sorry." Nicolas cleared his throat. "Not that son. Levi was only marginally successful in bringing you to safety. And he's injured. The boy can hardly stand up on his own. My son Joe has just returned from another mission. He can go with you."

To Levi's surprise, Isabelle stepped closer to him and placed a gentle hand on his shoulder. "Do you feel up to another mission?"

He smiled at her beautiful face in spite of himself. If he turned down this mission and let Joe take the credit for whatever might be accomplished, then Joe would be the next Sanctuary president. And Joe would be the one spending time with Isabelle.

But then again, maybe Joe was the better man for the job. Joe had more experience. And Joe could stand up on his own. Levi knew that if their mission failed because of his injuries or lack of experience, he'd never forgive himself. "My greatest concern is for your safety," he began.

"I trust you," she said softly.

Levi swallowed, a sick dread swirling in his stomach. He had the trust of the princess. But did he deserve that trust? Was he strong enough to keep her safe?

"Fine." His father circled around the table. "I want you two on the next flight to Lydia. I'll contact Prime Minister Emini and let her know you're on your way. We'll take in a separate team for backup, but I won't tell Emini, Valli or any of the generals about them. They will be waiting just out of sight to protect you if need be and to get you out of there if you get in over your heads. I won't have a repeat of your last adventure."

Isabelle didn't hesitate but turned to face Nicolas. "Thank you for your thoughtfulness. What's our cover?"

The Sanctuary president smiled. "You're the princess. He's your bodyguard. Unless your father or older brother steps forward, *you* are the heir to the Lydian throne. And I believe Lydia's laws stipulate that Parliament controls the coronation."

Isabelle appeared to take a moment absorbing the situation. Then she asked, "What about Valli?"

When everyone looked uncertain, one of the men who'd entered with Nicolas spoke up. "Should we request his cooperation? If the reason for your return is to investigate Valli, you'll need to get close to him."

"He's right." Nicolas nodded.

Isabelle still looked hesitant. "But can he be trusted?"

Levi let go of the table and placed a hand on Isabelle's arm, and if he leaned on her somewhat, she didn't seem to mind. "If the whole world knows you're under Valli's care, he'll know better than to hurt you. And if you feel you're in danger again, you won't have to rely on me to get you out of the country this time. We'll have a backup team at the ready. And we'll hold a press conference before you leave the United States. The whole world will know where you are, and they'll be watching."

The trust and determination that simmered in Isabelle's eyes sent Levi's stomach rocking. Or perhaps it was just the effort from standing up. Either way, a sick feeling crept up from his gut. He'd do his best to keep Isabelle safe and return the throne to her family. But would his best be enough?

"Then it's settled." Nicolas nodded with authority. "Isabelle, Samantha will get you everything you need. We can get you back home by the time the sun rises in Lydia."

Levi gave her what he hoped was an encouraging smile, then watched as Isabelle followed Samantha from the room. What had he just agreed to do? They were heading right back into the troubled world they'd worked so hard to escape. And he was in a lot worse shape now than he had been when they'd started out the last time.

"Lord, help us," he prayed quietly as everyone else left the room. "We're going to need a miracle. Possibly several miracles."

EIGHT

Isabelle felt grateful for all of Samantha's help packing. The woman was full of insights into Sanctuary's methods. She also seemed to know a fair bit about Levi.

"I wonder if Levi is up to this mission," Isabelle worried aloud. Although she hoped Nicolas had only been exaggerating, it had seemed as though Levi was hardly strong enough to stand up on his own. He'd certainly leaned heavily on her arm.

Samantha clucked her tongue. "Levi has no choice but to make sure this mission is successful."

"What do you mean?" Isabelle felt grateful for the supplies Sanctuary was providing for her trip. She made a mental note to pay them back when she was restored to her rightful role.

Assuming her family ever regained the throne.

"Levi's father is retiring next year. He'll appoint one of his sons as president after him. Everyone knows he favors Joe, even though Levi is older."

"Joe," Isabelle repeated the name. "That's the son he offered to send with me."

"Joe has more experience with military operations. He's a hero. Levi's just—" Samantha laughed "—a lawyer." She made a face as though the idea of Levi saving anyone was a ridiculous notion. "If I were you, I'd ask to have Joe accompany you, not Levi. I mean, the guy could hardly stand up."

Isabelle inhaled a sharp breath. Was she crazy to depend on Levi? But she knew she could trust him—and she hadn't been kidding when she had said they'd learned to work with one another. If Joe accompanied her, she'd have to adjust to working with him.

But Joe was apparently the more skilled operative.

And he could stand up on his own.

Sitting down in the nearest chair, Isabelle mulled over her options. If she was honest with herself, she had to admit she wanted Levi to go with her because of the way she felt about him. It was more than a simple matter of trust. Her whole world had been rocked on its side and her family ripped away from her.

And she was about to face the man who'd engineered her failed engagement. The man who was quite possibly in league with whoever had tried to murder her family.

More than a skilled operative, she needed someone to support her. Someone who could make her feel strong, who could reach out in the darkness and wipe away her tears.

She needed Levi.

Standing and continuing to pack, Isabelle told Samantha resolutely, "That's okay. I'll stick with the Grenaldo brother I know."

And then she tried to assure herself that she hadn't made a fatal mistake.

Levi was relieved to learn Sanctuary had arranged to hold Isabelle's press conference in one of the chapels at JFK airport. That would give them the opportunity to announce her survival to the world and then leave, providing a minimal window for the insurgents to reach her. He could only pray they weren't making a horrible mistake by making her whereabouts known.

He could tell Isabelle was nervous about the press conference also. They arrived well ahead of their scheduled announcement, and the chaplain ushered them into a small alcove to wait out of sight until it was time to make their announcement.

It wasn't until the chaplain had left and shut the door after them that Levi realized just how small the space really was. Isabelle stood next to him and had to look up to meet his eyes. He would have invited someone else to join them, but there really wasn't room for another person.

"It will be all right."

She gave him a small smile in return for his assurances. "I'm trying to trust God for that."

"Would you like to pray?"

Relief flooded her features and she placed her hands in his. "That would be the best thing."

Levi tried to think. "I'm sorry. My tired mind is having trouble formulating words."

"Mine, too." Isabelle sighed and closed the two inches that remained between them, resting her cheek against his upper arm. "But I believe God hears our prayers even when the things we pray for are too difficult to put into words."

"Then let's pray in silence."

Isabelle didn't respond. Levi could only assume she was already lost in prayer. Turning his own heart toward God, he focused on remembering all God's promises in scripture, even the promise of the passage from Ezekiel that Sanctuary claimed in its mission statement. "I will give you back the land," he murmured.

"I was just thinking that," Isabelle looked up at him.

Her brown eyes were warm under their thick lashes, and for a moment all Levi could think about was the kiss they'd shared earlier that day. It would be so easy to close the last few inches between them and kiss her again. So easy and yet so far beyond what he'd been called on to do.

When his father opened the door a moment later, Levi was infinitely glad he'd chosen not to kiss the princess. As it was, Nicolas Grenaldo raised an eyebrow at the way Isabelle was wrapped neatly in his arms.

Levi made no apology but stepped out of the room and away from Isabelle as she accompanied his father toward the lectern. Her hair was back up in its trademark high-piled arrangement, and she wore a simple pantsuit that looked elegant and professional.

The gathering of reporters was small enough to suit Levi. He didn't want a throng. Far from it. The news stations could share footage all they wanted once Isabelle was in the air. For her safety, he didn't want to have to deal with any more people than was absolutely necessary.

His father made the announcement—that Isabelle was alive and returning to Lydia to sort out what had happened there and try to determine if any of her family members had survived. When the inevitable deluge of questions for Isabelle began, Nicolas Grenaldo raised his hand.

"Her Majesty has endured a horrible ordeal. Your prayers and support are far more necessary than answers at this point. She will share more with you when she has more to share."

That silenced them.

Isabelle leaned toward the microphone. "I appreciate your concern. Please pray for the well-being of my family."

Thankfully, rather than another barrage of questions, a few considerate reporters clapped and the rest quickly did the same, showing Isabelle their support.

She took a step back, and Levi was immediately at her side.

"Ready?" he asked.

Her nod was slight, her royal smile still aimed at the reporters, but her words were clear enough. "Let's go."

Sleeping on the flight back to Lydia was more difficult this time, perhaps because her fears outweighed her exhaustion. Isabelle struggled to find a comfortable position in the tiny window seat.

"Worried?" Levi asked softly.

Isabelle had hoped he was sleeping. It would have been nice for one of them to be well-rested, at least. "I have a lot to worry about."

"You don't have to face Valli." Levi's expression was frank.

"I know." Isabelle studied his face, from the cuts that appeared to be starting to heal, to the bruises that were even uglier now. "But the world knows I'm alive now. They know I'm going to be in Lydia.

If Valli tries anything, he'll only draw attention to himself. There are too many eyes on Lydia right now for him to risk harming me under the circumstances."

"He might yet find a way."

She mustered up a smile. "That's what you're coming along for."

They fell into a somber silence, broken several minutes later by Levi. "Is this going to be too difficult for you?"

"I—I don't suppose—"

"What I guess I'm asking is—can I do anything to help? I mean, besides trying my best to protect you."

Isabelle's thoughts flew to the kiss they'd shared at the airport. But as her cheeks warmed with a deep blush, she realized that wasn't what he meant.

Levi must have sensed her discomfort. "Are there particular people or situations you wish to avoid? You mentioned not wanting to see Valli. Obviously that's unavoidable at this point, and I suppose your ex-fiancé won't be around—"

"I should hope not."

"And the scene of the—" He cleared his throat. "I'm sure you'll want to avoid…"

"Oh, that." If possible, Isabelle felt her blush deepen. "No, Tyrone's attack on me didn't take place in Lydia. We were in upstate New York, actually, at a place he owns in the Adirondacks. There's a riding stable near there, and it was such a peaceful place. I was just finishing college at Dartmouth, so it was only a two-hour drive away. I'd hoped to get to know him better. I had sensed for some time that something was wrong." She frowned, realizing she'd spoken more to Levi about that painful time than she'd shared with anyone in the two years since.

"I'm sorry."

"It's in the past. I got through that, and I suppose I'll get through this, too, with God's help. God has never let our family lose the nation of Lydia, not in almost two millennia. They've fallen back and lost territory and even gone into hiding before, but as long as the nation of Lydia has existed to bring glory to God, the Royal House of Lydia has never been snuffed out. And I pray we never will be."

Levi extended his hand toward her. "Would you like to pray?"

His offer was far too welcome to pass up, even if she wasn't sure how she'd react to holding his hand again. Their prayers in the alcove off the chapel earlier had been a great comfort to her, as had his close presence supporting her. She slipped her hands into his. The burns he'd sustained had finally been treated and were healing nicely, not that he'd ever let them slow him down.

"I'd like that." She dipped her forehead near to

his. This time the words came in whispers, in starts and stops, with Levi filling in requests for strength and protection, but she was finally able to give all her fears to God.

Levi was infinitely glad that Isabelle had managed to fall sleep. Their prayer time appeared to have eased her fears. He was grateful for that. Their mission was precarious enough without the added distraction of fear.

Though he'd hoped their arrival would be smooth, he saw immediately upon landing in the Lydian airport in Sardis that they wouldn't be that fortunate. News crews from stations around the world were clustered on the tarmac.

Isabelle met his eyes. "So much for staying off their radar."

Half a dozen soldiers made their way through the news crews.

"The second one." Levi pointed through the plane window. "Isn't that—"

"Sergio Cana, my brother's friend. The one who warned us at the Embassy."

Levi felt a moment's relief that the soldier hadn't been removed from his position. Then he wondered why not. Had he struck a deal with the insurgents to avoid a stiff punishment? "I'm still not sure we can trust him," Levi warned Isabelle as they prepared to disembark.

"I agree."

They descended the steps of the plane, and the next several minutes were a blur. Reporters shoved microphones at them, and Isabelle did an excellent job of ignoring them until they reached the door to the airport. But Levi had watched her ears growing redder, and she spun around in the doorway and faced them all.

"Where are all of you when I travel to Africa to dig wells? Where are you when I visit orphanages and hospitals in Third World countries? Twenty-four thousand children die every day from preventable causes. So why do you care so much about my family?" She gave them all a pleading look before she turned and hurried inside.

The soldiers led them to a waiting limo.

Isabelle balked at the sight of it.

"It's not—" he started.

But she shook her head. "All our limousines were destroyed in the attack. This one belongs to the U.S. Embassy."

"It looks unscathed."

"All the more reason not to trust Valli."

Isabelle ducked into the car, and he followed so closely that she no more than sat and he was seated beside her. She slipped her hand into his.

He wondered if she realized what she'd done. He gave her fingers a reassuring squeeze.

She squeezed back.

"You did a good job handling the media."

Isabelle blushed. "I shouldn't stir them up, I know, but they've never been on my side. They maligned me so badly when I broke off my engagement to Tyrone."

"You don't have to apologize," Levi assured her, giving her hand another gentle squeeze. "I thought you handled them very well."

Isabelle looked away through the window, and Levi got the distinct sense she was finished with the conversation. Had his words upset her? Or did she simply have so much else on her mind?

He felt her tense every time the limo paused, but they arrived at the Hall of Justice, as planned, to meet with Prime Minister Gloria Emini. Their footsteps echoed through the marble halls as they made their way to the Chamber of Parliamentary Session. Four of the six soldiers went ahead of them and two behind. When they reached the heavy wood-inlaid doors, the two head soldiers each pulled one open, stepping each to the side so the princess could pass.

Although their meeting was technically only to be with Prime Minister Emini, Levi saw the semi-circular rows of seats were nearly filled.

Isabelle had dropped his hand as they'd left the limo, but she stayed close beside him as they approached the prime minister.

Gloria Emini, an impeccably groomed, slender woman in her late fifties, stepped down from her usual post on the dais and welcomed Isabelle with open arms.

"Your Majesty." The prime minister hugged the princess. "It is such a relief to see you alive. Praise the Lord."

"Praise the Lord," Isabelle echoed, smiling graciously. "It's good to see you, too. Now, what do we need to do to allow Parliament to meet? Have you found a contingency to cover our current circumstances?"

Gloria Emini shook her head gravely. "The members of Parliament can, of course, meet unofficially at any time. But no official business can take place without the authority of the ruling sovereign, save the appointment of a new ruling sovereign."

Levi watched as Isabelle absorbed the news. He knew she'd been hoping some obscure rule would be uncovered that would state otherwise.

"Is there any way—" Isabelle met Gloria eye-to-eye "—any temporary status I could rule under that would allow my father to resume his rule if he is found to have survived the attack?"

"There is nothing, Your Majesty. The laws of Lydian succession are very clear. Once the crown passes from a sovereign ruler, it cannot be returned. It can only be passed along to another."

Levi was aware of the many pairs of eyes watching them carefully. The chamber was full, but no one made a sound, as all those assembled strained to hear the unfolding conversation.

"I would like to give my father more time. I believe he is likely still alive."

Gloria cast a grave look. "The fact that he has not made his whereabouts known does not sit well with Parliament. Almost two days have passed since the attack. I understand that the circumstances are grave and an attempt was made on his life. But he has a duty to rule his people. If he cannot fulfill that duty, Parliament has the right to name his successor."

"But I'm not ready to—"

"It isn't up to you." Gloria placed one hand on Isabelle's arm and dropped her voice. Levi had to lean in closely to hear her next words.

"There has been a request that the order of succession be revisited."

It took Levi a moment to grasp the meaning of the prime minister's words.

Isabelle looked stunned. "What? The rest of the royal family is absent. I'm next in line to the throne, the only member of the royal family—"

Gloria squeezed Isabelle's arm. "King Philip's grandfather, Alexander the third, had an older brother, Basil."

"Basil abdicated. He ran off to America with a Greek actress and died four years later."

"Basil had a daughter."

Levi could see a vein pulsing furiously in Isabelle's throat. He could hardly believe what he was hearing. It had to be a thousand times more difficult for Isabelle.

Though Gloria's expression was sympathetic, she didn't hesitate to press on. "Milo," she addressed the parliamentary clerk, "could you read to us the relevant passage from the Articles of Succession?"

Isabelle wavered slightly. Though he had been standing by quietly less than an arm's length from her, Levi took a step closer and placed a steadying hand at Isabelle's back. He wished he could do more to support her, but all of Parliament was watching intently, and he knew he had to look bad enough with the cuts and bruises on his face.

Milo stood at a large open book that rested on a raised podium near the front of the chamber. He cleared his throat. "The line of ascension is restricted to the natural legitimate descendents of Lydia, founder of the first church of Lydia, founding mother the kingdom of Lydia and servant of God. Primacy follows to the eldest natural legitimate descendent of the eldest natural legitimate descendent of most direct relation to our founding mother Lydia, the primogenitor of the Lydian line, without regard to gender, providing the heir is a willing ruler and individual of regarded faith."

When he had finished reading, Milo looked up

at the assembly and pushed his glasses higher on his nose.

Levi could feel Isabelle trembling, but she kept her voice strong as she spoke. "Who, then? Who is next in line to the throne?"

Movement near the side of the crowded room drew Levi's attention, and he turned in time to see Stephanos Valli step out from a cluster of members of Parliament.

Though he wished he could cover Isabelle's eyes and ears and whisk her off before she could hear what Gloria was about to say, there was nothing Levi could do but stand firm and pray.

Gloria Emini took a step back from the princess and gestured with her arm to Stephanos Valli as he joined their circle.

The prime minister cleared her throat. "There is an older natural legitimate descendent than you, Isabelle. Basil of Lydia has a grandson. Stephanos Valli."

NINE

Isabelle wanted to scream. For a moment she thought she might faint, but Levi's hand supported her back and kept her upright. She struggled to find her voice, more than aware that the members of Parliament were watching her and fully cognizant of their pivotal role in crowning the next ruler of Lydia.

"Stephanos Valli is not a citizen of Lydia." She wished her voice was stronger.

Milo cleared his throat from the podium. "He can become a citizen. He's lived in the country long enough to become a citizen right now. There is no requirement that the ruler be born a citizen."

"I see." Much as Isabelle wanted to protest that there ought to be such a requirement, the last thing she needed was to be found in contempt of the Articles of Succession. Knowing it was expected, she finally let her eyes fall from Milo the parliamentary clerk to Stephanos Valli, who stood smugly beside the prime minister, his beady eyes glittering.

"I, too, was shocked by this discovery." Valli's teeth glinted unnaturally white as he spoke. "But I have always followed the laws of Lydia during my many years of faithful service to this nation. Your father is obviously unable or unwilling to rule. Lydia needs a king. And if the law requires me to be king, who am I to refuse it?"

Isabelle had never been a violent person, but she was sorely tempted to slap the man for his ugly insinuations in front of Parliament. Not only was he clearly behind the attack, but now she understood his motive: to rid Lydia of anyone with a claim to the throne so the way would be clear for his succession. Her father, King Philip, was about six years older than Valli. As long as Philip was alive, Valli had no claim to the throne. What had Valli done to her father?

The man who'd tried to have her entire family murdered now extended his hand toward her.

To refuse it in front of Parliament would only turn people against her and win sympathy for Valli. No doubt that was part of why he offered it.

Poise and grace had been instilled in her since birth. She placed her hand in his.

He raised it to his lips.

She just managed not to cringe, leaning back against Levi's supportive hand at her back and reminding herself that she had to make nice to Valli if she intended to gather evidence against him— evidence that could save her family.

"My dear princess," Valli continued, still holding her hand. "I know you have been through a great deal. If I may, I'd like to invite you to stay at my residence behind the Embassy. There are many aspects of the current situation I would like to discuss with you."

Why didn't he want her staying in her own room at the palace? Isabelle stole a glance at Levi, and he raised one eyebrow slightly as though encouraging her.

She quickly realized what he was getting at. Though she would have preferred the comfort of her own room, Valli's invitation was ideal. She needed evidence against him. That was far more likely to be found at his residence, not hers.

"Thank you for your kind invitation," she nodded agreeably and was relieved when Valli finally dropped her hand. "I'm sure we have much to discuss." She turned to the prime minister. "How does Parliament wish to proceed?"

"We don't wish to rush into anything," Gloria Emini explained, "but at the same time, we feel a certain urgency to have an installed ruler, especially given the current turmoil. Lydia is in a state of unrest and cannot move beyond that state until the rightful ruler has been crowned."

"I understand," Isabelle murmured.

Gloria continued. "Please, meet with the ambassador. Discuss everything you need to. My office will contact you both in the morning."

Valli's smile broadened. "Shall we, then? I'll meet you at the Embassy shortly. You still have the car I sent for you?"

"Yes. And thank you." Isabelle didn't want to appear ungracious. She nodded at the prime minister and the clerk before exiting down the aisle as quickly as she appropriately could. The soldiers followed her to the limo.

As soon as Levi was seated next to her, she pressed her lips to his ear.

"I'd be surprised if this car isn't bugged."

"I agree." Levi spoke in a voice that was hardly more than a breath. "You did a fabulous job in there. I was ready to slug Valli."

Isabelle almost laughed with relief at his admission. "Thank you." She leaned against his shoulder as she spoke, as much for the comfort it offered as by necessity to keep from being overheard by any devices Valli might have planted. A shudder ran up her spine just thinking about the disastrous meeting. "Thank you for everything. I don't know if I could have done that alone."

"You're strong," Levi assured her, wrapping one arm around her shoulder and pulling her closer to him. His words, whispered in her ear, were little more than a breath. "Everything is playing out well.

Once we're inside Valli's residence, maybe we'll find something."

Isabelle pressed her eyes closed as she leaned close to Levi's ear. "But why? Aren't you suspicious? I don't doubt he'll have that place bugged, too. I'm bracing myself. What is he after?"

"All of Parliament knows you're staying with him. If anything happens to you at this point he'll be immediately suspect. He can't risk that at this stage. He's too close to getting what he wants." Levi's strong arm tightened around her, the last of his words raising to an audible level, as though Levi wanted to remind Valli or whoever might be listening to their conversation just exactly what they stood to lose if they tried anything against Isabelle.

They were nearing the Embassy. Isabelle let her head rest on Levi's shoulder a moment longer, basking in the comfort of his closeness. Too much had happened too quickly, and she feared everything was only going to get worse.

Entering Valli's lair was like entering a hornet's nest. Isabelle had no doubt she was still in danger, no matter what reassurances she'd been given. If Valli had indeed been behind the attacks on her family, no doubt her survival posed a terrible problem to his plans. If she'd died like he'd wanted her to, he'd likely have been crowned king already.

The car came to a stop under the carport that extended from the portico of the ambassador's residence, which was technically attached to the chancery, though the Embassy and Valli's residence were separate addresses. The same six soldiers who'd accompanied them since the airport stepped out of the SUV behind them and escorted them inside.

Valli had arrived just ahead of them, and greeted them. "I'm sure you'd appreciate a moment to settle in." He gestured to an attractive young woman in black slacks and a white blouse. "Calista will show you to your suite. And we have a room in the servants' quarters for your guard."

"My guard will stay with me," Isabelle said firmly. She forced a small smile to her lips. "Otherwise what is the point of having a guard?"

"The Embassy compound has impeccable security."

"I'm not concerned about threats from without," Isabelle didn't mince her words. Parliament was no longer watching, and she'd put up with enough from Valli already.

"As you wish," the ambassador's smile disappeared. "I've planned a late lunch. If you'll join me in twenty minutes, Calista can wait at your door to show you the way to the dining room."

"Thank you."

Isabelle and Levi trailed Calista up the stairs two flights and then down the hall. When they reached their guest suite, Isabelle dismissed the girl with a sympathetic smile. It wasn't Calista's fault she worked for such slime.

"I can find my own way to the dining room," she assured the girl. "I've been here before."

"Twenty minutes," Calista reminded them before hurrying off.

Isabelle and Levi quietly scoped out the suite. As she'd hoped, there were two bedrooms at opposite ends, each with their own bathroom, and a large living area between, complete with corner kitchenette and fireplace. Everything was decorated in a regal manner with tasteful appointments.

"I'll be right out." Isabelle excused herself to the bathroom. When she emerged a few minutes later, she found Levi sitting on one of two wood-inlaid white leather sofas that sat facing one another across a marble coffee table.

A few days before, she might have chosen a seat on the opposite sofa. But given the circumstances and the likelihood that the room was bugged, Isabelle slumped down on the sofa near him.

"Tired?" he asked in a normal voice.

"I don't know when I've ever been so exhausted." She didn't bother to whisper. The revelation would be news to no one. "And my feet are absolutely killing me." All the running she'd done in inappropriate footwear following the attack had left her feet aching.

Levi surprised her by gently lifting her feet onto

his lap and sliding off the ballet flats she wore before gently strumming her soles with his fingers. "Is that too much pressure?" he asked.

"It's perfect," Isabelle shook her head. "But you don't have to—"

"I'm here for your well-being." He silenced her. "If Valli was a decent host he'd offer you a spa treatment to relax you after all you've been through. Because he is not so thoughtful, this will have to do."

Isabelle couldn't help grinning at the thought that Valli's bug might have picked up Levi's comment. And his ministrations toward her feet made her feel infinitely better, too.

She watched his face as his eyes focused on her feet. How did the man manage to look so handsome, even with the bruises and cuts that marred his face? He had a bit of a fat lip on the side nearest her, and she found herself wanting to kiss his pain away.

Forcing her thoughts from that futile track, she reminded herself that any future romantic encounters with her gorgeous bodyguard were highly unlikely. After all, Samantha had been very clear about Levi's future plans. He was going to be the president of Sanctuary International if this mission was successful. And she might be Queen of Lydia, or possibly go back to being a princess, if she was very, very fortunate. Or Valli might have her beheaded.

Whatever her future held, she was quite certain it wouldn't hold Levi, at least not for very much longer. So the feelings she felt for him weren't meant to be acted on. Through his kiss at the airport, he'd taught her she was capable of that elusive romantic love that she'd wanted so much to find during her ill-fated engagement. For that, she would be forever indebted to him.

Besides, she realized as she looked at the clock on the mantel, they were expected in the dining room momentarily. "I suppose we should head downstairs in a few minutes."

Levi gently lowered her feet to the floor, then silently retreated to the kitchenette and washed his hands. Deciding she might as well wash up again, Isabelle joined him. Instead of handing her the sumptuous towel to dry her hands, however, he dried her hands for her, then took her hands in his.

"Let's pray," he mouthed silently.

Knowing they had little time to spare, Isabelle bent her forehead to rest against his. His prayers were more silent than a sigh, and she felt as though she understood him on a deeper level than mere words could communicate. She realized that when all was over and he was gone, she would miss the way they'd prayed silently together. It was something she'd never experienced before, but she'd found it to be marvelously sustaining when all she wanted to do was roll into a ball and cry.

She might have still been tempted to cry, but knowing what was ahead of her, she held her tears back. They were both up against insurmountable odds. At any moment the enemies surrounding them might turn on them and take their lives.

As Levi prayed, Isabelle felt her doubts fly away. Whatever was about to happen, God was with them. What had the verses for the Sanctuary pass code promised? "'I will give you back the land,'" Isabelle quoted softly.

Levi met her eyes as he whispered *Amen*. "Is there anything more I can do for you?" His expression was focused and sincere.

Instantly Isabelle recalled their kiss, but she shoved away the thought as she shook her head no. Levi had done so much to support her during this awful ordeal. She wasn't about to demand of him anything more.

"We'd best get going," she said aloud. Encouraged by their prayers, she headed for the door with Levi directly behind her, to face whatever Stephanos Valli had in store for them.

Levi's stomach churned. Nothing about the situation felt right. They were outnumbered in enemy territory, and though backup was only a phone call away, there was no telling what Valli might achieve before Levi's brother, Joe, and his team could arrive. Their principle defense was their vulnerability, and that was thin armor at best.

Sticking just behind Isabelle's right elbow, Levi

followed her down the stairs, half certain the chime of the grandfather clock in the foyer below was ringing out their death knell.

As they approached the open double French doors that led to the sumptuously laid table from which delectable Mediterranean scents wafted, Levi noted the two soldiers standing at attention on either side of the doorway. Levi recognized the man on the right as Sergio Cana, Alexander's friend who'd warned them away the first time they'd entered the Embassy.

Once again, Levi wondered what role the soldier was playing. Had he honestly gotten away with what he'd done? Or was he one of Valli's inside men? Could he be trusted?

As the princess crossed through the doorway, Levi slowed his steps, brushing near to Sergio. In that instant, the soldier's hand flicked out and nabbed his sleeve.

Levi's eyes darted toward him, though he hardly turned his head.

Sergio stood frozen but his eyes gestured away from the room.

At that moment, Levi understood. He wasn't invited to the dinner.

He took a step back and waited beside Sergio, watching intently as Isabelle was seated. For a moment she looked a little lost as she appeared to realize he was no longer beside her, but when she looked back, a relieved smile spread across her face.

Levi couldn't help smiling a little in return.

The meal played out like a performance, with dishes swept in and out by finely dressed wait staff, though the only two at the table were Valli and the princess. For her part, Isabelle was still wearing the wrinkle-resistant travel suit she'd worn for their flight. It wasn't terribly fancy, but on her anything looked stunning.

Something hard touched his hand. Levi realized he'd been so focused on watching the princess from the doorway that he'd hardly noticed Sergio inching surreptitiously closer to him.

He froze.

Then he seemed to hear that still, small voice Dom Procopio had talked about, telling him not to look at Sergio, nor to do anything to draw attention to what he held in his hand. Instead, his eyes still glued on the princess, he took the item that had been pressed into his palm, closing his fingers around it before he was able to identify what it was.

A key.

After several more minutes, once Sergio had slid silently back away from him, Levi tucked the key furtively into his pocket.

He still wasn't certain he could trust Sergio, but the scales had tipped a little further in the soldier's favor.

Other than a few polite questions about her flight

and comments on the food, Valli and Isabelle had spoken little. But as a tray of delicate baklava was presented to each with coffee, Valli sat back and took a sip before placing his cup on its saucer.

"You believe I instigated the attack on your family." There was no question in his voice, and his eyes didn't leave Isabelle's face.

Levi watched them both intently. He saw Isabelle's spine stiffen slightly and a hint of red color the tips of her ears.

Valli took another slow sip, replacing the delicate cup on its saucer without the slightest clink. "I assure you, Your Majesty, we are both pawns in a game being played by those far more powerful than either of us."

While Levi racked his brain trying to think who could possibly be more powerful than royalty and an American ambassador, Isabelle remained outwardly the model of composure, though he knew she had to be seething inside.

Her expression was demure, as though they discussed nothing more important than the phyllo pastry on her plate. "Why were there Lydian soldiers standing guard at the United States Embassy following the attack?"

"Why did you run from them?" Valli shot back.

Levi watched Isabelle weigh her words. Would she admit what Sergio had said? They didn't know whose side Sergio was on. If he was on their side, and his words had somehow not been brought to the attention of the powers against them, they couldn't risk giving him away by admitting what the soldier had said to them.

But what if Valli was telling the truth? What if he really was an innocent pawn? What if Sergio's comment had been meant to scare them away from the one man who could help them?

"You didn't answer my question." Isabelle lifted her coffee to her lips. How she held the cup steady, Levi couldn't imagine.

"I was away from the Embassy at the time, en route to the state dinner. The soldiers were dispatched for my safety."

"Then why are they still here?"

Valli gave a low chuckle and leaned forward in his chair. "My dear Princess, in case you have forgotten, I am the heir apparent to the throne of Lydia. Given the current state of unrest in our nation, the soldiers are here to guarantee my continued safety and yours."

Isabelle didn't like the look of the man who sat across the table from her, but she couldn't take her eyes off his face. Was Valli lying? Could he possibly be telling the truth? She wished she knew how to scent him out without exposing herself to more danger.

"If you and I are both pawns, then perhaps we ought to work together against those who would oppose the throne." The words surprised her even as they came from her own mouth. Was she crazy for suggesting Valli team up with her? He'd only ever betrayed and maligned her before. Yet, what had her father always said?

Keep your friends close and your enemies closer.

At least she knew enough not to trust Valli. She would choose her words with caution.

Valli's broad smile at her proposal did little to appease her fears.

"I had hoped you would be a reasonable woman. That's why I decided to give you the opportunity to entertain a proposal from an old friend of ours."

An old friend could have meant anyone, but the most obvious person they had in common was Tyrone Spiteri. Her former fiancé was anything but an old friend. An old arch nemesis, perhaps, but nothing like a friend.

But Valli *couldn't* be talking about Tyrone, could he?

Valli planted his elbows on the table and steepled his fingers in front of his nose. "I don't have to accept the crown. In fact, I fear it would be a burden. But I have allegiances, and if those allegiances are best served by my ruling as Lydian king, I will not hesitate to do so."

Isabelle couldn't think of anything to say, and her mouth felt as though it had been glued shut. She sat frozen in her chair, listening to Valli, wishing he would get to his point, and yet, at the same time, not wanting to ever have to hear what he was about to say.

"It may be more politically expedient for both of us if you were to be crowned. As we both know, if you were crowned queen, whoever you marry would then become king."

"Only as long as I am alive," Isabelle was quick to point out. She wasn't certain what Valli was getting at, but that detail needed to be clearly expressed. The last thing she wanted was for someone to think they could marry her, be crowned king and then kill her off. The law stipulated that only a direct descendent of Lydia could rule, so the spouse of the reigning king or queen had a title but no power.

But the way Valli's snaky eyes glimmered, she doubted that he saw the law as a major impediment. Laws could be changed.

The icy chill that crept up her spine left her frozen to her chair.

Valli raised one finger and a servant appeared from the doorway behind him.

"Bring our guest."

Isabelle's eyes flickered over to where Levi stood solidly behind Sergio. His compassionate eyes communicated strength. She willed her heart to stop pounding with such horrible dread.

And then her heart nearly stopped.

Tyrone Spiteri entered the room, his head held higher than ever, his proud smile nine-tenths smirk. His classic tall, dark and handsome features had once fooled Isabelle into falling for the billionaire ten years her senior. She had so hoped their love was real, that the attraction he claimed to feel for her was rooted in something deeper than physical beauty and prominent power.

But the more she'd learned about Tyrone, the less she'd found to like. He'd made a fortune in banking, lending primarily to the subprime market, but when financial crisis hit his country, instead of being sucked into its black hole of debt, he'd gotten inexplicably wealthier. Though charges had never been brought against him, Isabelle was certain he couldn't possibly have earned his wealth honestly or kept it legally.

Tyrone stood by Valli's side, his greedy eyes devouring her, even from that distance.

"My dear Isabelle, what a pleasure to see you." The edges of Tyrone's words were sharpened by all his broken promises, and they cut at her wounded heart. "I regret that our last meeting did not go as I wished, but I am confident today's meeting will remedy that."

Isabelle held fast to her chair. Her last meeting with Tyrone had been that fated visit in the Adirondacks when he'd tied her ankles to his four-poster bed and tried to rape her. If she hadn't nearly gouged out his eyes and left him blinded and bleeding, he would surely have gotten away with his crime.

He was threatening her. Again.

Much as she wanted to look to Levi for support, Isabelle wouldn't betray to Tyrone how much her bodyguard meant to her. If Tyrone suspected she felt anything for another man, he would destroy his perceived opponent.

For Levi's safety, she would have to play it cool.

"We trusted you to honor your promise," Valli's voice was silky smooth, but it spun like a web around her. "This time, we will not trust in honor alone. Parliament is eager to crown a new head of state as soon as possible, and I do not wish to make them wait. If you will agree to marry Tyrone Spiteri tomorrow, the two of you will be crowned king and queen, and I will step aside. If not, I will accept the crown, and Lydia will have no more use for you."

Isabelle didn't doubt that the threat she heard simmering under Valli's words was real. If she refused to marry Tyrone, Valli would have her killed for treason.

Tyrone advanced toward her, stopping midway down the table where a bowl of fruit served as centerpiece. He removed a blood orange and tore it open so that the crimson juice spilled down and pooled on the table. He took a bite of the fruit, but his eyes never left her face.

Then he gave a greedy laugh. "I look forward to tomorrow."

Valli raised his finger again, and when Calista appeared, he murmured. "Escort the princess back to her room."

TEN

Levi fell in behind Isabelle, who, he was impressed to see, strode from the room on steady feet, though her face had blanched white and he feared she was about to pass out. He kept close behind her in case he had to catch her as they ascended the two flights of stairs to their suite. The moment the door closed behind them, Isabelle crumpled into his arms, silent sobs coursing up through her as he held her securely and leaned back against the wall.

Finally the tremors shuddering through her stilled somewhat, and she pressed her lips near his ear. "I can't," she whispered, her words nearly silent. "I can't."

Levi understood. Valli and Spiteri were punishing her, trapping her and enjoying every second of their game. The two evil men clearly didn't see any way they could lose this time.

Isabelle gulped another stifled breath. "We shouldn't have come. Call your brother. Get us out of here. There is nothing I can do here to help my family. I'm only making things worse."

As her distraught words rose in pitch, Levi feared she might be overheard if the room was bugged. And he was more certain than ever that the room was, indeed, bugged.

His forehead followed hers until he could speak directly into her ear. "I have something."

She pulled back, and he watched her swallow another sob as her eyes met his, round with fear and red-rimmed.

His hand found hers and he gave her fingers a gentle squeeze, then tugged her toward the bathroom, pausing to switch on the television as he passed the remote. With the volume cranked up high, the added noise might help to drown out their whispers, but he wouldn't trust in that precaution alone. For all he knew, the room might hold hidden cameras in addition to bugs, but the bathroom was less likely to be bugged. Or so he hoped.

Guiding her after him, he stepped into the shower and pulled the curtain closed after them. Then he ran his fingers along the acrylic walls of the shower surround and up onto the plaster above, feeling for anything that might contain a hidden electronic recording or transmitting device.

Finally he inspected the shower head, unscrewing the nozzle. A trickle of water, probably left behind when the shower was used by the last guest, dribbled out.

Satisfied there was no hidden camera inside the fixture, he replaced the showerhead, but nonetheless kept his voice in a low whisper, using his body to shield the key from view as he pulled it from his pocket.

Isabelle bent close to him, questions clear on her face.

"Sergio slipped it to me while we were standing guard over the dining room." For the first time he was able to look at the thing, and he noticed tiny figures had been inscribed on the flat metal handle.

CV66O9C3

The letters and numbers had been written in with a fine-point pen, though he doubted the inscription was permanent. They would surely rub off from use in a short time. He quickly committed them to memory, even while he pondered what they might mean.

"Eight digits," Isabelle murmured, her voice nearly silent. "A combination of letters and numbers." She met his eyes. "It's a password."

"But to what?"

"Did Sergio say anything? Gesture in any way?"

"I hardly realized he'd moved toward me. He was clearly trying to go unnoticed."

Isabelle gave the key a studied look, turning it

over. There were no markings on the other side. "Can we trust him? Or is it a trap?"

Levi wished he knew the answer. For a brief moment, when Valli had made the claim about being pawns, Levi had almost entertained the idea that the man might *not* be in league with those who'd attacked the royal family. But when Valli had brought in that beast Tyrone Spiteri, Levi had been convinced that such a ruthless plan could only be orchestrated by someone whose heart held no goodwill.

"How can it be a trap?" He closed her fingers over the key, signaling he wanted her to keep it. "We don't even know what it's for."

"I would suggest that we try to feel out where Sergio stands, but there isn't time." Isabelle's words were practically silent, but Levi had learned to read her lovely lips. "We came here in hopes of finding some evidence against Valli. Perhaps God has provided us a way, through Sergio." She took a breath, and he could almost see her courage return. "Perhaps we should not run away quite yet."

He nodded his agreement. "Tonight when the lights are off we'll try the key in every door we can find."

She placed her hands on his shoulders and looked up at him, the frantic fear he'd seen in her eyes earlier now replaced by warmth. Affection.

They were too close. The scent of her hair, the

light cinnamon sweetness of the baklava she'd tasted, the warmth of her slender form against him were all overwhelming. He needed to put some distance between them.

And yet, how could he push her away? She'd been through too many terrors of late.

Her words were almost silent. "What about the password?"

Levi had to stop and think, to disentangle himself from his feelings for her. He had to remain objective, focused on their mission. What had she asked about? The password. "I can only hope we'll know how to use it when the time comes."

Isabelle peeled back the curtains that looked out on the courtyard garden between the chancery proper and Valli's residence. Lights that had glimmered in windows an hour before no longer shined. Levi had already scoped out the grounds. There were security cameras in the parking lot and courtyard, and dozens up and down the embassy hallways. But, as Levi pointed out in muted whispers, no one had stopped him as he'd passed up and down the halls scouting out the premises. They were guests. They had every right to be in the hallway. And with so many cameras, the odds were good security personnel didn't monitor every view at every moment. As long as they stuck to the shadows, they could avoid being seen. When they had to be in the open, they could pray no one was looking or that their presence wouldn't raise any alarms.

Smoothing down her black sweater over her black pants, Isabelle wished she could so easily squash the anxious churning in her stomach. She and Levi were already surrounded by their enemies. If they were caught in the act of investigating, there might be no escape. Levi had called his brother, Joe, who headed up their backup team. If Joe didn't receive a text from them by midnight assuring him everything was fine, he and his men would move in.

But so much could happen before midnight. Isabelle wondered if she was foolish to attempt to use the key and the password. She knew they were risking their lives.

But she also knew she had no choice, not if she expected to keep Valli from taking the throne. Once rule passed from her father, he couldn't reclaim the throne, even if he was still alive. Besides, Valli was corrupt to the core. There was more at stake than just the lives of her family members. Isabelle didn't want to imagine what would become of her country with Stephanos Valli as king.

Levi joined her beside the window, questions in his eyes.

With their room already in darkness, Isabelle didn't have to fear giving themselves away as she peeked the curtains open so that Levi could see for himself the dark windows across the courtyard.

The way was clear. They could proceed.

What little part of that evening she hadn't spent in fitful rest, Isabelle had committed to constant prayer. God had always protected the nation of Lydia, even through awful assaults before. She clung to the faith that He would be with them now.

Levi took both her hands and pressed his forehead to hers. She could feel the prayers radiating off him, though his lips did not move and he made no sound. Still, she knew they were united in purpose. Had she not been on the verge of nausea over what they were about to attempt, she might have given in to the affection she felt for him and the intimacy of the moment they shared.

Instead she took a deep breath and looked into his familiar eyes, which appeared gray in the darkness. She knew him well enough by now she didn't need light to see. She felt as though she knew him by heart and thanked God he was with her, certain she couldn't pull off their plan without his help. Levi was a gift. He was the only reason she was still alive.

As she had earlier when he'd shown her the key, she pulled her thoughts away from the distraction of her feelings for him. Now was not the time to explore how they felt about one another. Far, far too much was at risk.

Isabelle watched through the peephole in the door to their suite until the patrolling guards had passed well by. Then she slipped out the latex gloves Levi had brought from New York. He'd thoughtfully packed a kit of anything he'd thought she might need, including a flash drive for gathering evidence. They slipped into the hallway, closing the unlocked door behind them. Isabelle fingered the pocket on her slacks for the flash drive and cell phone she'd placed there. Both could prove to be invaluable.

As they'd already discussed in muted whispers, the two of them made their way silently down the stairs to the first floor. The chancery and ambassador's residence were only connected on the first floor, and the two intended to try the Embassy offices first. It seemed the most likely place to find evidence against Valli and the least likely place to be caught.

They kept to the shadows. Between draperies and pillars holding artwork and deep doorways set in thick stone walls, there were plenty of places for them to duck out of sight and listen whenever the slightest glint of light gave them cause to fear for their safety.

Once in the wide-open foyer of the Embassy, where they'd nearly been captured two days before, they held back in the lee of the wide staircase.

Fluorescent white streetlight shone in through the narrow windows in the doors and through the round window above them, spilling in an oblong puddle across the floor. It highlighted Levi's sharp features as Isabelle met his eyes, waiting. They both knew the next step—up the staircase to Valli's office.

The move would force them into the open.

The farther they went from their suite, the less opportunity they had of effectively using the excuse that they'd gotten lost, though there was little reason for anyone to believe they would need to leave their suite with its well-stocked kitchenette in the first place.

If they were caught, they would be in grave danger. It was that simple.

But if they failed to keep Valli from claiming the throne, whatever danger her family might currently be facing would only get that much worse.

Bolstered by that knowledge, Isabelle twitched a tiny nod at Levi, and they tiptoed hand-in-hand up the marble stairs.

Isabelle recalled from her visits three years before that the grand double doors at the top of the stairs marked the entrance to Valli's office. Light filtered into the hallway through a row of second-floor windows, through the open air of the high-ceilinged foyer, exposing their shadows. Isabelle jabbed the key in the lock and choked in shock when it slid straight in.

Her heart paused in its beating as she gave the handle a turn and it slid smoothly open.

That was easy.

Too easy?

Levi gave a nod and, as planned, stepped back behind the leafy expanse of a potted palm just beyond the doorway. He would stand guard, though neither of them had ever articulated precisely what he was to do if their discovery was threatened. Isabelle could only pray it wouldn't come to that.

Ducking inside, she found the office much as she remembered it from three years before. Everything was inlaid mahogany, from the bookshelves that lined the walls, to the massive desk that dominated the room, to the stiff leather visitor's chairs she'd sat in on her previous visits.

Now she slid into the plush leather seat behind the desk and found it to be of far more comfortable construction. Leave it to Valli to secure comfort for himself while forcing his visitors to sit on stiff chairs.

With a glance to make sure the window shades and curtains were closed, Isabelle slipped the key back into her pocket, slid out the slender flash drive she'd brought with her and wiggled the mouse of Valli's computer, glad for the gloves Levi had brought from the United States, which would prevent her from leaving incriminating fingerprints.

The monitor shimmered to life, revealing a backdrop of the Great Seal of the United States rimmed with block letters identifying the Embassy of the United States of America. Over the belly of the eagle, obscuring the red, white and blue shield, a window requested login information.

Isabelle hesitated. She wasn't authorized to tap into the Embassy network. But as she blinked at the glowing screen, it occurred to her that she didn't have to. Valli's login ID was already entered, and below it, ten black dots indicated the computer remembered his password.

Ten dots—two more than were inscribed on the key Sergio had passed to Levi. So that wasn't the password she'd memorized.

With a silent prayer she hit enter and came to a page filled with options.

Which was most likely to yield evidence that Valli had conspired to have her family assassinated? She clicked *Mail*.

Again, Valli's login, but this time, no black dots. She entered the memorized figures.

Incorrect.

She stared at the screen, disbelieving. The key had worked in the door. Why didn't the password work?

Isabelle heard a thump in the hallway and, unsure what else to do, ducked below the desk.

She listened to the sound of the door opening. Bright lights filled the room.

Levi wouldn't be so foolish.

Isabelle bit her lip. Yup, the excuse that she'd gotten lost in the building was never going to fly now.

Feet padded across the lush carpet until the shiny black shoes of the Lydian soldier uniform appeared behind the desk chair Isabelle had pulled toward her.

Sergio?

The odds were against it, and even if it *was* him, she didn't know if she could trust him. Maybe he'd given her the key to Valli's office just so she could get caught breaking in.

Besides, if the soldier was on their side, where was Levi?

Where *was* Levi?

Questions rattled her heart so hard Isabelle felt certain the soldier would hear its frantic pounding inside her chest. But an impatient huff later, the shoes pointed back toward the door.

The lights went out. The door clicked shut.

Isabelle crouched a moment longer. Had the soldier left the room? Solid inlaid mahogany on the side of the desk facing the room blocked any view she might have had in that direction.

Her thoughts raced. The feet she'd seen were distinctly too small to belong to Levi, even if he'd knocked out a soldier and stolen his uniform, which was preposterous anyway. She could only assume that Levi was gone and she was alone.

Fine. Her objective hadn't changed. She needed evidence against Valli and she needed it a week ago. Raising her head cautiously above the level of the desk, Isabelle scanned the dark room for a sign of the soldier.

Nothing.

Even the monitor had gone dark.

Levi awoke in darkness and groaned against the pain that radiated through his skull. Whatever he'd been hit with had not only knocked him cold, but also had left a trail of something sticky on his face, which made it difficult for him to open his eyes.

Blood?

He tried to touch the spot but found his hands wouldn't move more than a few inches in any direction.

The lingering smell in the pitch-black space was familiar. Sorting the scent from that of his own blood, he worked his head around the throbbing pain to name it.

The dungeon.

Yes, he'd smelled that scent two days before when he and Isabelle had broken in to the Embassy basement. So the chains that cuffed him to the wall were the ancient shackles he'd seen dangling from the stone wall then.

As his eyes adjusted to the dark, Levi saw a dim glow far off to his right and could just make out the echo of men's voices laughing. Was someone coming?

Levi tensed.

But after several long heartbeats, he realized the light hadn't changed and the voices had not drawn nearer. So they'd posted a guard on the other side of the door to the dungeon? He wouldn't let a couple of guards stop him from getting back to Isabelle.

Groaning, Levi got his feet up under him and lunged forward.

He felt a smatter of dust fall on the bare skin at the back of his neck.

The chains were old and rusty. The stones were only held together by centuries-old mortar; he'd chiseled his way through newer two days before.

Encouraged, he gave another mighty lunge forward, and the shackles dug into his wrists. But as crumbles of dust pattered against the stone floor, Levi felt encouraged. It might not be possible for him to tear the fetters from the old wall, but that wasn't about to stop him from trying.

Isabelle was up there. Alone. Undefended.

He lunged forward again with such force that his body rocked back, and his head landed hard against the stone wall. He waited a moment, wondering if the guards on the other side of the door had heard the racket he was making. But, no, their laughter still rumbled distantly, and he realized that at their distance, the sound of their own voices was enough to muffle whatever noise his chains might be making.

Sucking in a breath, he lunged forward again. It didn't matter, really, if escape was possible or not. All that mattered was getting Isabelle out of Lydia alive.

His father had given him a mission, and he intended to see it through. Another lunge forward left him panting for air. As pain racked through his body, from his throbbing head to his old injuries to the places where the shackles had begun to tear into his wrists, Levi wondered why he cared so much about being the president of Sanctuary International. Was it really worth going through all this?

Another lunge sent him rocking back, this time coughing against the dust he'd raised. Giving each cuff an experimental tug in turn, he found them still solidly anchored to the wall. It would take forever to pull them loose.

Closing his eyes, Levi pictured Isabelle's dark-eyed beauty, saw the smile that so easily sprang to her full lips.

And then he recalled his anger at the threats Valli and Spiteri had made against her.

He lunged forward furiously and was rewarded by a steady rain of mortar crumbling down onto his back. He wouldn't tear the shackles from the wall for his father. He would do it for Isabelle because he couldn't bear the idea of what would happen to her if he didn't get her out of Valli's grasp.

* * *

Isabelle wriggled the mouse, bringing the monitor to life again.

The red words continued to declare her login invalid.

Strumming her gloved fingers on the impeccably clean glass that covered the desk, Isabelle decided to check the inscription on the key again. Had she memorized the numbers incorrectly? It didn't seem like her to fail in something so important, but she *was* under a great deal of stress.

CV66O9C3

Isabelle stared at the numbers in the middle. She'd entered the *O* as a zero. After all, it was surrounded on either side by numbers. But what if it was the letter *O?*

How many tries would the computer let her have before kicking her off or sending some error message to Valli?

She typed in the figures carefully, using a letter instead of a zero.

Welcome, Stephanos.

Her sigh of relief was audible.

Shoving the key back deep into her pocket, she scanned the messages. The senders ranged from local officials to bureaucrats in the United States. Minutes from meetings, notes of addendums, corrections and official matters of state. Blah. The man led an even more boring life than she did.

Then her eyes landed on the name she'd been looking for.

Tyrone Spiteri.

She clicked the message and blinked several times, trying to make sense of the words from the email on the screen. The letters belonged to the English alphabet, but the words weren't any she recognized. Reading them aloud under her breath, she hoped to recognize the language, though it didn't resemble any of the French or Italian she'd studied.

Texetai paidion

Isabelle stopped short as the words left her mouth. Τεξεται παιδιον was Lydian for "give birth to a baby." So the words made sense after all. The Lydian language, a close cousin of Greek, used the Greek alphabet. That was why she hadn't recognized the words because the message was composed using the English alphabet.

The email was in Lydian, the language abandoned a century ago when the progressive leaders of their small nation had adopted English as an official language—a strategic move that had bolstered trade and improved their economy. Hardly anyone in Lydia spoke Lydian anymore, certainly not anyone under the age of ninety, although as princess, Isabelle had been taught the language that was still considered a vital part of her people's heritage.

Valli and Tyrone had apparently decided to encode their messages in Lydian by transliterating the Lydian messages phonetically into English-alphabet-based words, substituting the English letters of similar phonetic sound.

Sneaky. There were probably only a couple dozen people in the whole world who knew Lydian and a smaller number still who would know enough of it to work out the contents of the message. Their strategy reminded Isabelle of the Navajo code-speakers from World War II, who'd used an almost-dead language to move messages through enemy lines. Whatever Tyrone and Valli were up to, they had gone to great pains to conceal the details.

By reading the message under her breath, Isabelle was able to hear the message and translate its meaning in her mind. Even so, she quickly realized she'd entered their conversation well into its progress. They were talking about someone having a baby but she couldn't tell whose or why they cared. Neither man struck her as the nurturing type.

Exiting the message, she noticed a search field for the email account and entered "Spiteri." For her efforts, she was rewarded with a host of messages between Tyrone and Valli, dating back long before her engagement.

Much as she wanted to scan through the messages and learn what they were up to, she didn't have any time to waste. She'd already taken too long, and translating the coded messages would take far more time than she had to lose. Quickly she jabbed the flash drive into a port and began copying all the messages to a document before storing them on the drive she'd inserted.

While she bagged the messages, she decided to do another search. Tyrone didn't have any control over Lydian soldiers and neither did Valli. And she didn't buy for one second the ambassador's excuse for why Lydian soldiers were guarding the U.S. Embassy. They answered to one of the three generals. She did a quick search for David Bardici.

Pay dirt.

Not only were there several recent messages from the general, but the other two generals, Corban Lucca and Marc Petrela, were included in the missives. The messages had all been placed in the trash file after having been opened, but to Isabelle's relief, their contents were still viewable. From what she could tell, Valli's system must have been set up to delete trashed messages after one week. None were any older than that. A quick glance at the contents demonstrated that these emails, too, were encoded in transliterated Lydian.

For a moment, Isabelle debated whether to read the emails. She might not have much time. Someone could walk in on her at any moment. But then again, she might have all night, and she'd be devastated if anything happened to the flash drive and she had no idea what the messages said.

Clicking open an email dated six days before— prior to the ambush on the royal motorcade but after the message to Albert was intercepted—Isabelle read the coded words aloud quickly, just enough to give her an idea of what was being communicated.

The men knew about the message that had been intercepted and about the death of Albert and someone named Besnik. She could only assume Besnik was the other man who'd been floating in the Mursia. Anyway, from the sound of it they were both dead, and none of the four men included in the email were happy about that.

Their final question rang ominously through her mind. *Does this change our plans?*

She'd intended to stop reading after one email, but she quickly opened the next and got her answer. They were going to go through with it. Apparently all four involved knew what "it" was because details weren't given, only the promise of more to come.

Isabelle knew she didn't have time to translate any more. But she'd gathered enough from those messages to know she was on the right track. She'd have to sort out the details later. There simply wasn't time now.

Copying all the general's emails together with sender and recipient information as rapidly as possible to a document, she banked them on her storage device. A quick check of the device confirmed the documents had been successfully stored. She deleted the contents of the documents she'd made and then the files themselves before logging Valli out of his email. An expert might be able to dig up what she'd done on the computer, but by then she hoped to be long gone.

Isabelle slipped the flash drive into her pocket that held the key and padded silently across the carpet to the door. She slid it open a crack.

No one was in sight.

She darted through and ducked into the shadow of the potted palm.

Levi was nowhere to be seen, but she noticed a small red streak on the white marble floor. She'd seen enough of that substance recently to guess with confidence what it was.

Blood.

ELEVEN

The second shackle tore a six-inch rock from the wall when it finally pulled loose. Levi bent double, catching his breath. He didn't have time to free the shackle from the rock. He'd just have to drag it behind him.

Levi was relieved to find the doorway to the catacombs that he'd knocked through the dungeon wall two days prior appeared to have gone unnoticed, shielded as it was in its shadowy corner by construction debris and piles of boxes. He had nothing to light his way—the men who'd captured him had taken his cell phone—but as he recalled from his earlier trip through the tunnel with the princess, the jaunt across the street to the cathedral was a brief one. He'd simply have to feel his way and be very careful not to miss the stairs up. Otherwise he might end up wandering the catacombs indefinitely.

Trailing his hand along the wall and moving as quickly as he dared, he prayed the whole time that the soldier who'd knocked him cold hadn't discovered Isabelle. She hadn't ended up chained next to him. No, they'd surely chain her to Spiteri instead.

He increased his pace and nearly fell forward as the wall gave way under his hand.

Stairs.

Ten minutes later he opened one of the front doors of the cathedral, stepped outside into the night and slid a thick brochure between the jamb and the door, stopping the locking mechanism from engaging—just in case he decided to break back in. The front door would be much faster than crawling around through the catacombs. Then he made his way down the steps of the cathedral, across the street and up the front steps of the Embassy. He stood in the shadow of a marble pillar and peeked inside, his thoughts running fast ahead of him.

He didn't know of a way to get into the building. The windows of their suite looked out onto the courtyard, which was surrounded by the building. He didn't know how to get inside the courtyard, either, enclosed as it was by walls on all sides. At least the marble pillar shielded him from the view of the nearest security camera.

How many guards did Valli have? The soldier who'd knocked him out had probably had help dragging him off and chaining him up. And he knew they'd posted a guard of at least two men at the dungeon door. How many guards were left? And what might they be doing now?

Capturing Isabelle? Searching their suite? It would be the next place he'd go if he were the soldiers.

The soldiers who'd captured him had taken his phone. Now how would he contact the backup team and let them know the princess was alone, unguarded, likely already captured or on the verge of being taken prisoner? If he didn't contact his brother by midnight, Joe and his men would show up and probably walk right into a trap if something wasn't done before then.

A movement inside the Embassy foyer caught his attention. A dark figure descended the white marble stairs. A soldier? Had they spotted him? It was impossible to see much in the darkness, but then the figure passed through the beam of light from the round window above.

Isabelle!

Levi strummed on the glass inset in the door with his fingers, trying to get her attention.

She glanced his way, fear stark on her face in the white light.

Tapping frantically, wishing he had a way to let her know he was friend, not foe, Levi tapped out the old shave-and-a-haircut.

Isabelle must have realized a dangerous enemy wouldn't bother with something so silly, because she trotted over to the door and peeked through the window. Relief flooded her face as she recognized him.

Unsure whether the door had an alarm that would activate, Levi wondered if he should discourage her from opening it. She didn't give him long to consider the question—she pushed open the door by the slam bar and nearly fell into his arms.

Levi didn't hear an alarm, but that didn't mean there wasn't one going off somewhere. Besides, surely the soldiers were somewhere in the building, looking for the princess even now. He took her hand and pulled her across the street, grateful he'd thought to obstruct the lock on the cathedral doors.

Isabelle spilled through the door into the cathedral narthex after him, practically on top of him as he paused, trying to decide which way to run. He steadied her with his arms.

"What is this?" She lifted one of the chains that dangled from the shackles still attached to his wrists. The other had a good-size chunk of stone that the lodged bolt had refused to let go of.

"Shackles."

"From the dungeon?"

"I've had a busy night. Do you still have your phone?"

She pulled it from her pocket and handed it to him. "What happened to yours?"

"Soldiers." He dialed the number for his brother.

"You don't think they'd chain me up but leave me my phone, do you?" As he spoke, he led the princess down the hall toward the offices, away from the front doors where anyone might stumble upon them.

While the call rang, Levi asked Isabelle, "Did you get anything?"

Her bright eyes were answer enough. "Yes." She pressed a flash drive into his palm.

Levi slipped the drive securely into his pocket as his brother answered the call.

"Glad you finally called. I was about to send in the cavalry."

"We need a lift."

"Ready to head home, then?"

"Yes. Where can we meet?"

Joe suggested a nearby park with a wide-open area large enough to permit landing a helicopter. "Do you know the place?" he asked Levi. "How soon do you think you can get there?"

"Give us twenty minutes." Levi hoped to reach the spot sooner than that, but he wasn't sure how many soldiers they might yet encounter, and he didn't want Joe arriving too soon. If the soldiers spotted the helicopter before Levi and Isabelle reached the park, they might never get on board.

"See you then."

Levi handed the phone back to Isabelle. "If we

become separated, call the last number dialed." He pulled her down the hallway.

"You don't think—"

"I'm just trying to cover our bases."

"So what's the plan?"

"We need to get to Idylia Park. My brother's team will pick us up there."

Isabelle tugged on his hand, slowing him to a stop. "How are we going to get there?"

"The catacombs have an exit through a manhole one block from the park."

The princess shivered visibly and shook her head. "They chained you in the dungeon, remember? Do you really think they were just going to leave you there? I bet Valli is headed down there right now, ready to interrogate you or knock you off himself."

Levi didn't doubt her theory. The man already seemed to hate him. He'd only be that much more furious once he realized the princess had slipped out of his grasp. "You're afraid they'll find the entrance to the catacombs?"

"Yes. And if we're in there, it won't be difficult for them to track us down. There's nowhere to hide in the catacombs. Besides, we don't even have a flashlight."

"But the city is crawling with soldiers."

Isabelle looked thoughtful. "We need to get the information on that drive to someone who can help us. I would have emailed it directly from Valli's account myself, but that would have left an electronic trail on his account—and if he was logged in elsewhere he would have known immediately what I was doing and probably where I was, too."

"Right. Let's find Dom." Levi tugged her down the hall toward the offices.

"Dom Procopio?"

"He had a computer in his office."

Isabelle sighed her relief. "Good. We'll email the documents, then catch up to your brother. Do you think you should call him and warn him that we might be late?"

"Late? Who said anything about being late?"

Levi spotted the door to Dom's office and gave the wood a gentle rap. When they'd been in the office two days before, he'd noticed the sofa in the corner was the fold-out kind, and the pillows atop it looked as though they were made for sleeping, not decoration. If his guess was right, the old deacon spent as many nights in that office as Levi spent in his, which was most of them. And with soldiers on the lookout for royal sympathizers, Dom would likely keep his head down.

A shuffling sound inside the room preceded the glow of a dim light, and then Dom's weary face peered through the cracked-open door.

"Again?" He pulled the door wide, sounding pleased to see them. "I saw on the news you were back in town. Say, Your Majesty, good speech to the media, too. I was surprised they had the guts to show it." As he spoke, he pulled them inside and closed the door behind them.

"It was the only sound bite I gave them." Isabelle cast a smile to where the computer in the corner sat, its screen alight with the latest Lydian news. "Could we use your computer? We have some files we need to forward."

"Anything I can do to help."

Levi took the seat and quickly input relevant Sanctuary email addresses before pulling the files from the flash drive and sending them off with a quick note explaining the contents.

"You'll have to warn them they're encoded," Isabelle told him as he typed.

"Do you know how to break the code?"

"It's Old Lydian, transliterated with the English alphabet. Does Sanctuary have anyone who knows Lydian?"

"My grandmother might still remember some. She's ninety-one years old and lives with my folks in New York."

"See if she can decipher any of it. Otherwise it will have to wait for me. I don't know of anyone else outside of my family who knows the language. The tutor who taught me died years ago."

As Levi sent off the files, he addressed Dom. "We need to get to Idylia Park in less than ten minutes."

"That's a couple kilometers from here," Dom

warned him. "And don't you two need to stay out of sight?"

Isabelle placed her hand on Dom's arm. "That's why we were hoping you could help us."

Dom shook his head. "I'm surprised they've left me alone after those two thugs followed us in the delivery truck. I can only assume they never made it out of the river." He looked thoughtful. "I'd offer the truck, but the roads between here and Idylia Park are so narrow that it would hardly be faster than walking, if we could get through at all."

"You haven't got another motorcycle around, have you?" Levi asked.

"Motor *scooter*," Dom corrected him. "For puttering around town."

"It's faster than walking. You don't mind if we—" Levi stopped short of using the word "borrow." It wasn't as though they'd be bringing it back. Dom would have to go find it himself.

"Commandeer my scooter?" Dom's eyes twinkled with merriment as he finished Levi's question. He was probably already picturing the two of them trying to putter away to safety. "You're welcome to it." Digging out a set of keys, he peeled one from the ring and handed it to Levi. "This way."

Isabelle held tight to Levi's shoulders, peeking behind her at the Lydian soldiers who stood on the far corner. The scooter hummed quietly in the other direction, and the men, busy with their conversation, didn't even glance their way.

She had to hand it to Dom. His little bike kept them in stealth mode. Too bad it seemed to struggle so much with the hills.

"Should I get off and push?" she offered as the bike groaned up a particularly steep hill.

"Just pray," Levi murmured.

When the park came into view, Isabelle felt hopeful that they might actually make it in time. Then she heard the drone of a helicopter and saw a pair of soldiers on the next corner turn their heads to the sky, looking for the source of the sound.

"You should have told your brother to come by motor scooter. It's quieter," Isabelle chided Levi as he parked them in the shadow of a van beside the curb nearest the park.

Both of them slid off the bike, and Levi tucked the key under the seat as Dom had instructed him. He took her hand. "Those bushes," he nodded. "Stay low."

They darted toward the shrubbery as the helicopter above came into full view.

Levi kept one hand on her shoulder. "Wait for it. The second they touch down, we'll make a run for it."

Isabelle met his eyes and nodded. The poor guy still had shackles dangling from his arms, and she had yet to ask about the huge stone he was pulling like a ball and chain. She'd have to tease him about it later.

Assuming they survived.

The helicopter hovered over the clearing beyond them. Just as its landing skids kissed the grass, Levi gave a nod. "Keep your head down." They darted toward the opening cabin door.

For a moment, Isabelle allowed herself to believe they were going to make it.

Then sod kicked up near her feet, the sounds of the gun drowned out by the whir of the rotors. Isabelle nearly screamed.

"Up! Up!" Levi screamed, gesturing to the helicopter to take off again.

Isabelle felt his hands at her waist as he tossed her through the waiting door.

The landing skids rose from the earth as he continued to shout. "Up! Take her up!"

"Levi!" Isabelle screamed. The bird was six feet off the ground already and soldiers were closing in.

If he stayed behind, he'd be dead in ten seconds. It was a wonder he hadn't been shot already, but the soldiers appeared to be holding their fire. For now.

"Grab the landing gear!" She leaned out the door after him as though she could pluck him off the ground herself. His words from two days before shot through her mind—his instructions to leave him behind in the alley if he passed out. In a snap, she realized that's what he was doing: he had every intention of letting them take off without him. He'd secured her safety. He cared nothing about his own.

Isabelle threw her upper body out the cabin door. Perhaps if Levi thought she was ready to dive out after him, she could convince him to try to get on board. Someone behind her had hold of her legs and was shouting something, not that she could hear over the roar of the rotors.

Flinging his arm forward, Levi swung that big stone rock in the air and it cleared the landing skid, the weight of the rock carrying the chain after it, wrapping the chain tight around the metal as the whirlybird kicked up in earnest.

They shot straight into the sky, and whoever had hold of her legs pulled her back inside the cabin.

Levi dangled below. Isabelle figured they'd have to find a safe place soon to land so he could climb aboard. It would only be a matter of time before those ancient chains gave way. They'd already had their strength tested.

She panted for breath. The man who'd pulled her in began to slide the door shut.

"No." She stopped him with a hand on his arm and peeked out. Levi's strained expression swept into view as he swung below them like a pendulum. "Can't you pull him in?"

"We can't risk you falling out." She recognized the man who addressed her as Joe, Levi's brother, who'd she'd been briefly introduced to before they'd left New York. The brothers shared many features, including their zeal for ensuring her safety.

"If you don't want me to fall out, then hurry up and pull him in." She mustered up as much royal authority as she could infuse into her breathless voice. "Before I have to pull him in myself."

Joe gave her one look and must have decided she meant business. He leaned toward the pilot. "Put down on that next island. Get her just above the ground. Levi's tangled on the skids. We'll have to untangle him before he can board."

A moment later they hovered over smooth sand. Isabelle recognized the island as part of the archipelago that extended from the city of Sardis out into the Mediterranean. The islands were uninhabited, save by the many visitors who sailed out to enjoy the beaches during the warm summer days. But at this hour of night their stretch of white sand was deserted.

Joe hopped out and, after a few tense moments, Levi's face appeared. When Joe climbed back aboard a second later, he scowled at his brother.

"You threatened the safety of the princess." The younger brother accused, his words falling just short of *I'm telling Dad.*

"I threatened my own safety," Isabelle cut in while Levi caught his breath. "I wasn't about to leave him behind to get killed."

But Levi didn't seem interested in sorting out

who was at fault. "Get us to Rome. We need to be on the next flight to New York."

"You got it." Joe disappeared to join the pilot. There was some radio back and forth, but Isabelle's attention was on Levi, her hands sweeping over his arms and his face, assessing his injuries.

"How are your arms? Your wrists look terrible."

"Nothing's broken," he began to explain, just before Joe poked his head back their way.

"Are you sure you want to head to New York?"

Levi stared up at his little brother. "Why not?"

"They've just announced Stephanos Valli is being crowned King of Lydia at ten o'clock in the morning."

"Tomorrow morning?" Isabelle asked, aghast.

"Technically, it's this morning. The coronation is in less than ten hours."

TWELVE

Levi saw the realization of defeat pass over Isabelle's features.

"If Valli is crowned king, my father will be never be able to reclaim the crown." Her dark brown curls had come loose from her sleek ponytail, and they bounced prettily against her cheekbones.

"His reign might be deemed invalid," Levi assured her. "If we could prove he murdered your family."

"If Valli is the ruling king, he won't let his reign be deemed invalid." She looked at him with aching sorrow in her eyes. "And there's no way we can stop the coronation now. Parliament has already made clear that Valli is next in line for the throne."

"But the evidence you gathered," Levi hurried to reassure her. "It will prove he conspired to assassinate the king."

"Will it?" Tears welled in Isabelle's eyes. "I hardly had time to translate any of it. I don't know what those messages contain. Besides, it's all a moot point. Even if we could prove what Valli did, once he claims the throne, we'll never be able to take him to court."

"Perhaps not in Lydia," Levi acceded. "But the UN Security Council may be convinced to intervene." He scooted a little closer to her and laid one hand on hers.

"Not before ten o'clock this morning. We can't even get to New York that quickly, let alone get an audience with them. 10:00 a.m. in Lydia is 4:00 a.m. in New York. Everyone will be asleep."

"They're awake in New York now," Joe stuck his head back toward them, obviously having listened to their conversation. "We'll have Dad give them a call. If the Security Council issues a warning to the Lydian Parliament, they can delay the coronation. By the time we reach New York, you could have a case ready to bring before the Council."

Levi looked at his brother. "The Security Council rarely acts that quickly."

"They've been watching the situation closely," Joe assured him. "They know something's afoot in Lydia. They'd probably appreciate someone letting them in on what it is."

Levi sighed, the wheels of his tired mind spinning. He'd have to dictate a formal appeal to the Security Council, explain exactly why they were requesting the coronation be halted. The Council would only agree to intervene if specific criteria were met. Levi was fairly certain he could make a solid case, but it would take time to spell out the specific points.

Then he'd have to get Isabelle working on decoding the emails. His ninety-one-year-old grandmother couldn't be expected to do it all herself, especially because she probably didn't remember much of the old language.

"Fine." He looked at his brother pointedly. "I need to talk to Dad. I need a laptop for Isabelle, and I'd like a pair of bolt cutters waiting for me at the Rome airport." He held up his wrists. "I'm not going to make it through security looking like this."

Isabelle watched him with wide eyes. "Do you really think it's possible?"

"It just might be—as long as there's a chance, we'll do whatever we have to. We've been through too much to give up now."

"But—" Isabelle shook her head "—it's the UN Security Council. We can't just walk in spouting something about coded emails. At the very least we'll need an expert in international law."

Joe laughed and punched his brother in the arm.

"What's so funny?" Isabelle looked warily between them.

Realizing he probably should have told her sooner, Levi explained. "That's the kind of lawyer I am. I specialize in international law."

* * *

Isabelle looked up from the computer screen and blinked her weary eyes. It had been a long night already, and they were only a few hours into their flight to New York. She'd hoped to grab a little sleep on the flight, but the messages she'd been working on wouldn't let her rest. For one thing, she still had many more messages to slog through.

And for another, she found their contents chilling.

Tyrone had been planning to do away with her family as far back as four years ago, before he'd even talked Valli into contacting her. His plan then had been to marry her, get rid of the rest of her family and then become king when she was crowned queen.

He'd realized, of course, that he wouldn't have any power. Because he wasn't a descendent of their founding mother Lydia, he'd never hold more than a token title. But he'd already figured a way past that.

The plan had been for the two of them to have a child together. Their offspring would be a direct descendent and therefore able to reign. But as long as that child remained a minor, they'd need a regent ruling in their stead.

That was where Tyrone had planned to get his power. Once she'd provided him with a child or two, he'd have her locked in a tower somewhere, or killed off, and then rule in the place of his children.

With a sick feeling in her stomach, Isabelle realized *that* was why Tyrone had been so eager to get her into his bed—especially when he'd suspected she wasn't planning to go through with the wedding. He'd hoped to make an heir, even if he had to take it by force.

Isabelle shuddered. How Tyrone thought he could sneak an illegitimate child past Parliament she could only imagine, but the man seemed to think himself capable of outsmarting everyone, so she didn't doubt he'd been confident of getting his way.

With a sigh, she closed the document containing messages between Tyrone and Valli. There was still more to be translated, but she had more than enough to prove Valli had been conspiring with Tyrone Spiteri to assassinate the royal family.

Now she needed to catch up on how the generals were involved. There was still much more to their complicated plans, and she didn't have long to sort it out.

In the seat beside her, Levi had kept up a steady stream of typing, preparing documents for his father to advance to the Security Council. As she understood it, the Council had called an emergency special session to determine whether to intervene in the Lydian coronation.

Her heart warmed at the sight of his focused features. The bruises on his face were mellowing, and though they'd managed to remove the thick shack-

les from his wrists, his lower arms were scuffed
and bruised. Typing had to be painful, but he didn't
falter.

He must have felt her looking at him because
he glanced up, his fingers still typing. He looked
back at the screen of his laptop, then did a double
take and stopped typing. The hint of a smile on his
weary face sent her heart skipping.

"I'm resting my eyes," she explained.

"Have you been able to learn anything?"

"More than I ever wanted to know." Figuring it
would be helpful for his case, Isabelle explained
what she'd learned about Tyrone's plans to rule
through royal offspring.

"He was planning to kill you then and reign in
the child's stead?" Levi shook his head. "He would
murder the mother of his own child just to increase
his power? That's so cruel I can hardly fathom it."

"I don't believe Tyrone ever let me see the full
extent of his thirst for power, but the glimpses I got
were enough to scare me away. He was a ruthless
businessman and he hated anything that kept him
from getting his way—usually laws meant to protect the innocent. I'm sure he thought if he was king
he could change the laws to suit his desires."

"And kill anyone who stood in his way."

Isabelle rubbed her temples, the whole ugly mess
making her head throb. "I need to sort out how the

generals were involved. My father trusted them. How could all three of them betray his trust?"

Levi's hand covered hers. "I'm afraid your research will show you more than you ever wanted to see of the potential for evil in the human heart."

The simple touch of his hand did wonders for her wounded soul. For a moment, she allowed herself to consider the less urgent questions that had plagued her since the ambush of the royal motorcade. "How can anyone be so convinced of their own right to power that they would kill innocent people to get it? What makes them so evil?"

She thought Levi might brush away her question and tell her to get back to work, but instead he leaned slightly closer, pain simmering in his eyes. "Greed is a powerful force. All of us have the potential to be sucked in. I have seen good leaders brought low when the taste of power became more than they could resist, and they hungered for more and more."

"My father is powerful. And he never—"

Levi's finger brushed her lips, the slight touch stilling her words. "Your father appointed those three generals. They reported to him."

Her eyes narrowed, but the tip of his index finger still rested at her lip, so she remained silent.

"I don't know what you will find when you read those messages, but I want you to be aware that it might be something you don't want to hear. If your father knew his generals could be bought—"

She shook off Levi's touch, unable to sit silent any longer. "My father is a good man," she whispered. "He wouldn't plot anything against his own family."

"I don't believe he would do anything to hurt you or your siblings. But he may have gotten in over his head." Levi's eyes were full of sorrow. "No one is completely good except God alone. The rest of us must wrestle daily between choices of good and evil. I know your father strives to always choose good. But that's not always possible."

Isabelle sucked in a shaky breath. She understood what Levi was getting at. She didn't like it, but she understood. Her father had been the one to agree to her marriage to Spiteri. She'd only gone along with it because she trusted her father and had naively believed in the promise of love. "He may have had to compromise in the past."

"And that compromise may have come back to haunt him." Levi's eyes fell on her computer screen, and Isabelle looked there, too. The puzzling combinations of letters streamed on, their hidden messages promising disillusionment. But she needed to know the truth, even if the truth was ugly. It was the only way she could help her family now.

She offered Levi a slight smile. "Thank you."

His head tipped in question.

"For warning me," she explained. "And for helping me find the truth in the first place."

The stiff navy blue suit jacket covered the injuries on his arms, but there was nothing Levi could do to cover up the damage to his face. He didn't like facing the UN Security Council looking so rough, but he had little choice. He was exhausted and not nearly as prepared as he would have otherwise insisted on being. But he had an audience, and that was more than he might have wished.

The Security Council had advised Parliament to postpone the coronation. Parliament had agreed. Now all he had to do was convince the world that this interruption had been worthwhile.

Stepping out of his private quarters into his office, Levi felt his breath sucked from his lungs at the sight of Isabelle sitting in a chair, waiting for him.

She wore a simple but well-fitted charcoal-gray skirt suit, with an ivory blouse peeking out from underneath, its fluttery collar adding a slight feminine touch to her otherwise strictly professional ensemble. Shimmery gray hose and black loafers completed the look.

Her thick hair was parted at the side and combed back into a loose knot, from which several thick curls escaped—he suspected strategically. Her dark eyes captured his, and there was nothing he could do to keep from smiling.

"Shouldn't you be resting? You haven't slept in two days."

"I could ask you the same question." She rose and joined him on his way toward the door. "And how could I sleep when the future of my country hangs in the balance? Besides, there may be questions only I can answer."

Levi struggled to breathe as they made their way down the elevator and recognized the swelling in his heart as an unfamiliar heady sensation that had only ever afflicted him around the princess. She was the woman of his dreams. It was too bad they each belonged halfway around the world from the other.

And after today, if things went well, he wouldn't have reason to see her again. Perhaps then he would regain full use of his intellectual faculties.

Until then, he would have to testify before an under-slept UN Security Council, with a distractingly gorgeous woman at his side. And if he did well, his father just might be convinced to let him be president of Sanctuary International after all.

They ducked into the limo Nicolas Grenaldo had insisted on hiring for the princess, even though Levi suspected she might have been more comfortable in a cab. He pulled her hand into his. Her fingers felt cold despite of the warm day.

"Nervous?"

"I'm beyond nervous." She turned her lovely eyes toward him. "But right now, the nerves are the only thing keeping me awake."

He grinned. "Me, too, I'm afraid. If I start sounding like an idiot, just elbow me and I'll be quiet."

She honored him with a laugh. "You have to promise to do the same for me. I'm so tired now I might say anything."

"Just speak from your heart and you'll be fine." He gave her hand a gentle squeeze. "From what I've heard, several Council members have expressed interest in hearing your side of the story. And I don't doubt the media will be eager to report your every word."

Isabelle made a face. "This is their chance to redeem themselves then. If the media can sway the public against Valli, I promise to be nice to them in the future."

"No more sound bites about the dying children of Third World nations? I'd be disappointed if you gave those up."

"I didn't say I'd give them up—" her smile told him she was teasing "—only that I won't be so snarky about it."

Levi laughed, the affection he felt for this tough, humble woman more than his weary heart could bear. Once her safety had been secured, he would have to stay away from her. It was that or risk acting on the feelings he felt for her, and there was no way he could do that to her after all she'd been through.

Isabelle entered the Security Council chamber in the United Nations building with wide eyes. She'd seen pictures of the place before, but they hadn't captured how vast and regal the room seemed or how tiny she felt staring up at the mural of a phoenix rising from the ashes. She knew the bird was meant to represent the world reborn after World War II, but she couldn't help but hope it might symbolize her own country's rise out of ruin.

"'I will gather you from the nations and bring you back from the countries where you have been scattered,'" she quoted the passage from Ezekiel under her breath.

Levi leaned close. "'I will give you back the land again.'" He gave her a meaningful look as they were seated, and though she knew the words were a promise from the Lord, she realized they were Levi's promise, too. God had worked through Levi to keep her safe and was still working through him to return the nation of Lydia to the descendents of Lydia. She had much to thank him for.

Soon the president, one of the fifteen members of the Council who, as Isabelle understood it, rotated through the role on a month-by-month schedule, opened the meeting with thanks to the other members for meeting on such a compressed timeline.

Besides the fifteen members, the room was filled with aides, and Isabelle recognized the officials from Lydia who represented their tiny nation in the UN.

Isabelle listened in fascination as the meeting began. As Levi predicted, the members were eager to hear her side of the story, including how she'd survived the initial attack.

As Isabelle recounted the events, trying to keep everything in order as it had happened in spite of the blurring effect of the near-sleepless adventure, she found herself giving credit to Levi time and again. Well, it was really no surprise. He'd saved her life. Dramatically. Repeatedly. Appreciation welled in her heart as she spoke.

When she reached the part in her story about reading Valli's emails, murmuring spread through the crowd. She hadn't bothered to include all the lengthy and confusing details of Sergio passing them the key and the password written on it. She'd been invited into Valli's household. Did she need a warrant to procure the evidence she'd gathered? Not in Lydia, not given the circumstances. But would the Council interpret things that way?

After she'd told her story, deliberations began in earnest. She kept hearing the phrases "act of aggression," and "threat to peace." The words gave her hope. From what Levi had explained to her, Isabelle understood that if the council agreed that the insurgents had committed an act of aggression that threatened the peace both in her nation and the surrounding nations, then they could be moved to intervene.

As the representatives discussed her testimony, Isabelle got the impression that several of them were sympathetic toward her family after all that had happened. The next question surprised her.

"Princess Isabelle, how do you wish us to proceed?"

She felt her eyes widen, and her poor tired mind was so stuck in shock she couldn't think of anything to say for a moment. When she glanced at Levi, he winked at her.

That sent a charge through her system. "I would like Stephanos Valli removed from his position and investigated further. Also, Tyrone Spiteri." She'd explained to them the emails, and the plot regarding the baby. State record would prove the previous assault charges, which he had finagled his way out of with minimum charges. "He should be investigated and held."

Heads nodded solemnly around the circle. "And what about the crown?"

"I suppose that's up to Parliament." Isabelle felt emotion welling up, and she fought to keep her voice steady. "Could you please ask them to put off crowning anyone until they've made a thorough and diligent search for my father?"

The president of the Council nodded solemnly. "We will break for lunch and discuss the details of carrying out your requests this afternoon." His attention turned to Isabelle. "Your Majesty, from what I understand from your story, you have not had a chance to sleep in some time. Might I recommend you get some rest? We will try to have your world back on its way to being right by the time you awake."

The tears she'd tried so hard to suppress throughout her testimony now flowed in silent trails down her cheeks. "Thank you."

Isabelle awoke and glanced at the clock. Shortly after midnight. She could have rolled over and slept through till morning, but she was far too curious to learn what had happened since she'd returned to Sanctuary headquarters.

Slipping on clothes from among the things Sanctuary had provided for her, she headed down the hallway to Levi's office. As she might have expected, the halls were void of activity. Though there were surely people still working somewhere in the building, they were behind closed doors.

The door to Levi's office was open and a barrister lamp glowed at his desk. Isabelle rapped on the door and Levi's head popped up from behind the dark computer screen.

"I'm sorry," she apologized as he rubbed weariness from his eyes. "I didn't see you sleeping there."

"I'm not supposed to be sleeping." He stood and circled around the desk, gesturing for her to have a seat. He took a chair that sat at an angle to hers. "I was trying to take care of a few things, but sleep caught up to me."

"You need your rest."

"Not as badly as I need to keep you safe."

His voice creaked with care, and Isabelle felt his sincerity steal her breath. In spite of the tired lines that cradled his eyes and the stubble that had returned to his chin, the man was handsome. Isabelle realized she seen him in all manner of facial hair configurations. They were like an old married couple.

The thought goaded her. She hadn't come looking for him so she could dream about a future that wasn't to be. She'd come to learn the future of her country.

"What did the Council decide?"

"The United Nations has asked Valli to voluntarily return to the United States for questioning. He's on his way to New York now. They've issued an apology for his actions. Everyone is hoping that with Valli out of the picture, if your family members are in hiding somewhere, they'll feel safe enough to make their survival public."

Relief coursed through her, tempered with a

strong dose of reality. "I fear Valli may be just the tip of the iceberg."

"I don't doubt you're correct. We'll need to you finish translating those emails at some point."

"I could work on that now."

"No. I need you to pack. We're sending you to a safe house."

"A safe house? Are you coming with me?"

"No. There are too many things for me to do here, and you'll have a rotating team of guards. You don't need me anymore."

Isabelle felt his words hit her like a slamming door. Samantha had warned her. Levi just needed one high-profile, successful mission under his belt. Then he could be president of Sanctuary after his father. He didn't need her anymore.

She felt her heart start to tear away from the safe spot it had nestled into. "When will I see you again?"

"There is no further need for you to see me. Sanctuary will take care of your needs until the situation in Lydia has been resolved and it is safe for you to return there. The Council has already discussed the likelihood of providing a peacekeeping team if necessary."

Isabelle shook her head. The Council's plans were wonderful—more than she'd hoped for, really—but one stark fact had stuck in her ribs and wouldn't let go. "When can I tell you goodbye?"

"Now." His face had turned cold and he'd stopped meeting her eyes, instead glancing back at his desk as though eager to get back to work. "You can pack a bag. I'll ring Samantha and she'll escort you to the car. The guards have been assigned. We've all just been waiting for you to wake up."

Isabelle rose from her chair and waited for Levi to rise from his. At the very least she wanted to hug him. He didn't move. His face was turned toward the work on his desk. "Levi?"

"I have work to do." He barely glanced her way and didn't stand.

Emotion caught in her throat, but Isabelle stifled her disappointment. She was a princess, after all. She wasn't going to beg Levi to hug her goodbye. Her voice wavered only slightly. "Thank you for everything you've done for me. I'll never forget you."

His face was still pointed away from hers, but she saw his jaw twitch. Was he angry with her? Impatient? She had thought she'd learned to read him, but now she felt at a loss.

He swept one hand down his weary face and nodded. "Goodbye."

So that was it then. She'd been dismissed. Isabelle knew too well how visits worked. It wasn't her place to linger.

"Goodbye." She closed the door behind her as she left.

THIRTEEN

Levi fumbled with a pencil and snapped it in half.

He couldn't catch his breath. Pushing his chair back, he raised his arms over his head and stretched, trying to force wakefulness into his exhausted body, to ease the tight pain in his chest, to convince himself that their parting hadn't been awkward.

But who was he kidding? She'd been going to embrace him, and he couldn't let her. He could hardly work up the voice to speak without betraying his emotions. If he'd gotten his arms around her again there would have been no letting go, not without confessing everything he felt.

And where could they possibly go from there? Even if she returned his feelings, which by rights she shouldn't, because they'd only just met and the world knew she could do far better than a workaholic, underpaid, nonprofit international lawyer— even if she felt something toward him, what could possibly come of it?

She was a princess and likely soon to be queen.

He lived half a world away, on the verge of finally inheriting the post he'd worked his whole life to fill. No, confessing how he felt would only make things worse.

So why did he feel like scum for not telling her he loved her? There was nothing to be gained by it. Nothing but heartache.

He turned from his desk and headed to bed.

That's what he'd do. He'd sleep it off. Maybe once he was fully rested he could convince himself he was making the right decision.

Besides, he was going to need his sleep. Once Valli was brought in, Levi was going to be a part of the initial interrogation team. He needed to find out once and for all who had been behind the attacks on the royal family. And then he was going to do everything in his power to bring those parties to justice.

Maybe he couldn't tell Isabelle that he loved her, but at least he could keep her safe and give her back the throne of her people.

It was raining. Water streamed in fat rivulets down the windows of the SUV from a gray sky. Dawn had broken some time before, but the clouds obscured the sun.

Isabelle tried to tell herself she was glad. Her enemies were being brought to justice. She was headed somewhere safe—near Buffalo—where she could rest up and maybe form a plan for locating her missing family members. Her heart burned inside her as she thought about her brother and sister and their parents. She believed they had to be alive somewhere. That faith kept her going. For the first time in three days, things were starting to look up.

Isabelle felt miserable.

She would have liked to settle back and rest, but she'd been stuffed in the backseat between Samantha and a bodyguard, with two more beefy guards occupying the front bucket seats. She didn't even feel as though she were free to cry, but the sky seemed to be doing enough of that for her.

The thought tilted a small smile at the corner of her mouth, and she felt the peaceful hand of God holding her, crying for her when she was too drained to weep for herself.

I will gather you from the nations and bring you back from the countries where you have been scattered, and I will give you back the land again.

The ancient words soothed her soul. God was faithful. He kept his promises. Though the ambush had tested her faith, Isabelle felt secure in trusting that justice would win out in the end, even if the end was a long time coming.

Through the swishing wiper blades Isabelle could see road signs splashing bright green ahead. She knew enough about the geography of upstate New York to understand their route. They'd take I-81 to

Syracuse, then turn west on I-90. It would have been something like a seven hour drive, if it hadn't been for the thick early-morning traffic. Samantha had already called back to Sanctuary to warn them they were running behind schedule.

Isabelle read the signs. I-81 would continue north and connect with I-90 East. They'd hop on 690 to connect with I-90 West.

The 690 exit slipped past.

Isabelle watched it go. She wished she had a map or something. The driver wasn't using GPS. She shifted uncomfortably. I-90 East loomed ahead of them.

The wrong exit.

The wrong way.

The driver steered them into the lane for I-90 East.

Isabelle cleared her throat. "Aren't we supposed to be headed west?"

"Just taking a little detour." The driver didn't take his eyes off the road.

The guard beside her must have felt uncomfortable, too. "Levi said no detours. No stops until Buffalo, except to get gas, which we already did."

"I need to use the facilities." The driver's voice was harsh.

The guard in the front passenger seat shook his head. "You should have gone when we bought gas.

You knew the instructions. Besides, you should have taken 690 to I-90 West. It's way back there."

Samantha cleared her throat. "Look, boys, there's been a little change of plans. Trust your driver. He knows what he's doing. Don't you all want to stay safe?"

"But the safe house is—" the front seat guard started to turn his head.

"Don't move," Samantha barked.

"Please don't move," Isabelle echoed, her eyes following the object in Samantha's hand. "She's got a gun."

"That's right." Samantha's eyes glittered. "And I'm not afraid to use it. So we're just going to take our little detour and you two are going to keep your mouths shut, or I'll shut them for you."

Isabelle didn't dare make eye contact with either of the two innocent guards. She didn't even know their names, but if they tried to do anything to save her, they'd probably be shot.

It hardly seemed fair.

It wasn't fair that Samantha had the only gun, either. The agent and the driver were apparently confederates, which left Isabelle with two guards who just might be on her side. Three against two. The odds were almost in her favor—if it hadn't been for Samantha's gun and the fact that the SUV was now headed in the wrong direction, to an unknown destination where Levi wouldn't be able to find her. And there was no saying how outnumbered she'd be once they arrived.

Levi was briefed by two men from the team who'd escorted Valli in.

"He's eager to cooperate. He'll give us evidence against Spiteri if it means we'll go easy on him."

It fit with what Levi knew of the man. Ruthless *and* spineless. A useful combination, at least for today. "What's the status on Tyrone Spiteri?"

The two exchanged glances. Levi got a bad feeling.

"The United States doesn't have any authority over him," one of the men admitted slowly. "I think they're watching him."

"*Watching* might not be entirely accurate," the other corrected. "He's—ah—"

"Missing?" Levi filled in for them.

They nodded, apology written across their faces. "But there's a UN peacekeeping team on the ground working with the Lydian Parliament. I think they're trying to locate him."

The other man held up a photograph. "Also, we've intercepted this. Not sure exactly where it was taken. Someone's cell phone camera. It will likely go viral."

Levi squinted at the grainy image. There was no mistaking the face in question, though Levi had himself been mistaken for the man a few days before. "Prince Alexander? Isabelle's brother?"

The man nodded. "You'll note he appears injured." He pointed to reddish streaks on the man's face. "That would be consistent with surviving the attack."

For a moment, Levi considered forwarding the photograph to Isabelle. She'd want to know right away if her brother was alive.

Just then a man came to the door. "We're ready."

"Coming." The picture could wait. With Spiteri at large, Valli's testimony was more important than ever. If he could give them information that would give them the authority to capture Spiteri, all the better. Until Spiteri was behind bars, Levi wouldn't rest—because Isabelle wouldn't be safe until Spiteri had been put away for good.

All too soon, Isabelle suspected where they were heading. The Adirondacks. She felt a churning in her gut. No! They couldn't be headed to Tyrone Spiteri's place, could they?

But why else would Samantha have a gun? If Samantha was on her side, wouldn't she have simply explained to Isabelle the change in plans? The only possible reason she hadn't was because she couldn't—because she knew Isabelle wouldn't consent to going along then.

One thing was certain: Isabelle couldn't let them

reach Spiteri's country estate. Something told her she'd never get out of there alive.

She thought about her phone, which was still in her purse. Was there any way she could call for help? But it would take too long to explain the situation to the state police, even if they were aware of the situation in Lydia.

No, she needed someone who'd understand right away what was needed. Someone she could be certain would follow through on her cry for help.

She needed Levi.

"I thought we were stopping for the facilities," Isabelle said in an innocent voice.

"He was lying," Samantha snarled beside her.

"But I really need to use the facilities." Play dumb, play dumb.

"You went before we left," Samantha reminded her, but she didn't sound quite so convinced herself. Isabelle had seen the woman drinking coffee earlier. She might not be the only one who would appreciate a pit stop.

"You can come with and bring your gun," Isabelle offered. "I promise not to run away."

Samantha's lips pressed together in a thin line. She was considering it.

"Fine. Let's pull over at the next available stop." Samantha turned the barrel of the gun toward Isabelle. "But you're not leaving my sight."

Fortunately the restroom had several stalls. Samantha insisted on taking the stall right next to Isabelle's. She had her gun out of sight but had made it clear she could use it on a second's notice.

Isabelle pulled her phone from her purse. As far as she knew, Samantha was unaware she had it. Fortunately, she'd insisted on entering Levi's new number for the phone that replaced the one the soldiers had taken when he'd been captured at the Embassy.

Knowing she'd have only seconds to compose her plea for help, she typed quickly.

help sam is dirt

"Let's go!" Samantha shouted.

Isabelle flushed and sent the message. It wasn't much, but it was all she could do. She'd meant to say Sam was dirty, but she didn't have time to add the "Y" or any further explanation—like where she suspected they might be headed. But Levi needed to know he couldn't trust Samantha. Beyond that, he was on his own to find her—if he could.

Now she'd just have to pray Levi saw the message soon.

Valli was talking in circles. Levi wondered what the man was trying to do—other than irritating his interrogators, of which he was doing a fine job. It was almost as though the man was stalling. But what could he possibly stand to gain that was more important to him at this point than cooperating for a reduced sentence?

"What do you know about Tyrone Spiteri's involvement in the plot to kill the royal family?" Levi asked, deciding to take a step back and broaden the line of questioning.

"Spiteri wasn't involved in the plot to kill the royal family."

Levi froze. He'd read the emails Isabelle had translated. Spiteri had wanted the royal family dead. And Valli had instructed the generals to make sure that happened—even to the point of having Alfred kill Isabelle if the missiles didn't take care of it.

Was Valli stupid enough to lie under oath? No, he was a weasel and a rat, but he wasn't stupid.

"But Spiteri was poised to benefit if the royal family died."

"To a point."

Levi wanted to reach across and shake Stephanos Valli's head. The man was being painfully obtuse. "Spiteri was poised to benefit if every member of the royal family died, with the exception of Princess Isabelle."

"Yes."

"So the plot to kill the royal family wasn't engineered by Spiteri, although he was aware of it."

"Yes."

"Spiteri wanted Isabelle alive."

"Yes."

That explained why the men who'd been after them hadn't simply shot them on sight. Spiteri had instructed them to bring Isabelle to him. Levi's stomach plummeted. "Where is Tyrone Spiteri now?"

"I don't know."

The man gave him a look that sent chills up Levi's spine. Where *was* Spiteri? What was he doing? And what would he do if he got his hands on Isabelle?

Something vibrated softly near his leg. It took Levi a moment to pull his thoughts from the line of questioning and realize the unfamiliar sensation was caused by his new phone.

He pulled it out.

One new message.

Levi clicked view.

help sam is dirt

Fear shot through to his heart. It took him a moment to recognize the number. Isabelle's phone? Was she not getting along with Samantha? Or was something bigger going on?

Spiteri was talking more about the generals. Levi would have loved to stay to hear it, but he feared he might not have time. "Excuse me." He ducked out of the room, phone still in hand and punched in her number.

His finger froze above the send button. There was that still, small voice nudging him to stop.

But why? It didn't make any sense. He needed to

call Isabelle and make sure she was okay. His finger wavered above the button.

Then he snapped his phone closed. Right. If she was in trouble and he called her, he might get her in more trouble. All someone would need to do was look at her phone and they'd find she'd sent him a message. And if she really did need help—if Samantha really was dirt, as the message implied— then giving away what she'd done would ruin the only advantage she had.

Instead, Levi opened the phone and called his father. "Has Isabelle's car reached the safe house yet?"

"No. Samantha called earlier to report they were delayed in traffic."

"Has Spiteri been located?"

"No one can seem to find him." Nicolas Grenaldo paused. "Is everything all right?"

"How well do we know Samantha Klein?"

"She's worked for us for years."

"Yeah, and Alfred was Isabelle's bodyguard for four years." Levi hurried toward the door. He needed to move quickly. Isabelle was in trouble. And Tyrone Spiteri was still at large. "I need a helicopter and armed men. Call the state police."

"Why?"

"Spiteri has Isabelle."

"You're kidding. Where?"

Levi paused at the street. It was raining. He

thought about hailing a cab, but traffic was heavy and the Sanctuary Offices were less than a mile away. He broke into a run, as everything Isabelle had told him about Tyrone's previous assault on her hit him like the rain that fell from the gray sky. "The Adirondacks. He has a summer home there. A two-hour drive from Dartmouth, near a riding stable. Find it for me. Thanks."

He snapped his phone closed and picked up his pace to a dead sprint. Isabelle hated Spiteri. She feared him. And for good reason.

Levi couldn't let Spiteri win.

Two armed guards met the SUV by the garage. Samantha darted from the car through the rain to where Spiteri stood under the garage awning and threw herself into his arms. Isabelle watched in horror as her former fiancé exchanged a passionate kiss with the woman who'd been holding a gun on her the whole trip. If possible, it made her feel even more betrayed. And it did not bode well for the result of this visit.

"All right, out of the car," Samantha barked, holding open the front passenger door.

The guard exited with his hands in the air. "I'm just a paid guard, Samantha. I'm not on anybody's side."

"I'd love to believe you, but I've seen you act honorably too many times before. And I can't risk you turning hero." She pointed the gun at him.

Isabelle winced.

"Tie him up," Samantha shouted impatiently, as though the other men standing by were supposed to have read her mind.

The next guard's exit was much the same. When the two burly guards were bound, Samantha gestured with the gun again, and Isabelle lowered her shaky legs from the backseat, giving the bound-and-gagged guards a wistful look. It would have been nice to just be bound and gagged.

She was pretty sure her visit wouldn't be so pleasant.

Samantha fell in behind her and prodded her forward with the gun.

Tyrone Spiteri smiled down at her. He had a way of smiling that was not at all friendly. "So, Princess, we meet again. When are you going to accept that the two of us were meant to be together? Each time I have to come find you, I just get more upset." The smile turned into a fierce growl. "You don't want to make me upset."

He led her inside the estate. Isabelle recognized the Arts and Crafts style architecture and the white-painted woodwork that she'd found so cheerful and comforting on previous visits. Now it held only ugly memories.

"Sit." Tyrone pointed to a chair and sat in the one

opposite it. Samantha kept the gun trained on her as she perched on the arm of Tyrone's chair.

Isabelle looked around the room, hoping to spot some means of escape, but none presented themselves. Besides, she'd have to get past plenty of armed men to get away. But they were on the first floor, and she knew the way to the front door. Maybe...

"You have rejected my offer before." Tyrone's words jerked her thoughts away from escape. "That was stupid. Now I am in a bad mood and I will not be so nice to you." He'd always had a rough accent. She'd found it exotic when she'd first met him, but now it only made the man sound that much more sinister.

"Here is the deal—you marry me and bear my child, or I will kill your family."

FOURTEEN

"We only have four men," Joe informed Levi as he entered the front doors, shaking off the rain, out of breath from his sprint to the building.

"Why?"

"Dad was thinking about what you said—about the possibility that Samantha might have turned. We both agreed we only wanted men we were sure we could trust."

Levi weighed their options. Trust or manpower? Which would be more important? He wasn't sure what he was up against, but he knew he was tired of being betrayed. "But the state police are going to meet us there, right?"

"Dad's going to get in touch with them next."

Levi knew they wouldn't be able to do anything to Spiteri without the police on their side. If Sanctuary agents stormed the place and captured Spiteri themselves, the agents could be accused of breaking and entering, even kidnapping, and Spiteri could end up going free on a technicality. They couldn't risk that.

"We need them on our side—"

"We'll have them in place by the time we arrive."

"Okay, fine. Do we have the location of Spiteri's estate?"

"Yes. Dad's getting us satellite images. We'll have to plan our attack while we're in the air."

"Let's get moving." Levi hurried down the hallway as he spoke.

"Aren't you going to change out of your suit?"

Levi thought about all the enemies he'd fought while in his tuxedo and with Isabelle in an evening gown, no less. "Are you kidding? This is casual for me."

"My family is *already* dead."

Tyrone threw his head back and laughed. It wasn't a very comforting sort of laugh.

Isabelle shivered.

"Do you really expect me to think that you believe that? We both know no bodies were ever identified."

Aware of the possibility that Tyrone might be able to help her locate her loved ones, Isabelle decided to play for all she could get. What did she have to lose? If nothing else, she'd be killing time. "But none of them have ever come forward. So what makes you think they're alive?"

"Your brother is in North Africa. Your sister is in Milan."

"And my parents?"

Tyrone shrugged. "They are in the care of General Lucca."

Isabelle's mind swirled. Was it even possible? Could her family have survived the blasts? Much as she wanted to believe it was true, she knew better than to trust Tyrone. She tempered her hope.

"Do you have proof of that?"

"You have my word."

Isabelle knew how much Tyrone's word was worth, but she decided not to mention that. No sense angering him further. "If I agree to your terms, you'll help reunite us?"

"I will do everything in my power."

His words sent chills chasing through her veins. The man had power, she'd learned that much. Where he got it from or at what cost, she couldn't say.

"And if I don't agree?"

"Then I will take what I want, and things will not go so pleasantly for you."

Isabelle swallowed. Things weren't going to be pleasant either way. Might as well make the guy think she was trying to cooperate. "What is your plan?"

"First things first. To discover if you are able to bear my child. If not, I will have to negotiate a deal with your sister."

"Are you sure you want to marry me? I thought you and Samantha—"

"What happens between me and any other woman is none of your concern!"

"But if we're married—"

He completely disregarded her protests. "First, we will see if you can conceive. I will give you three months, starting now." Spiteri rose from his seat.

No! Isabelle had to keep him talking. "The Lydian laws of succession state that in order to be crowned king or queen, an individual must be a *legitimate* descendent. That means the parents have to be married before the child is conceived."

"I do not believe that is what that means."

Isabelle had to force herself not to roll her eyes. The man was so used to getting his way, he thought he could change the meaning of words and laws. It didn't surprise her too much. "You can ask Parliament what they think it means. I'll wait." She crossed her arms over her chest.

Spiteri didn't call Parliament. Instead, he crossed the room to Isabelle and grabbed her roughly by one wrist. "Parliament doesn't know when anyone was conceived. If we make a baby, then I will marry you. It would look bad if I had to leave you for your sister so soon after we marry." As he spoke, he pulled her toward the stairs.

Isabelle knew what was up there. The bedroom where he'd assaulted her before. She wondered if the eye-gouging defensive maneuver would work a second time.

"Samantha!" Spiteri called over his shoulder. "Bring the gun! I want to make sure the princess doesn't go back on our agreement."

Though she hadn't agreed to anything, she figured that was probably a moot point in Tyrone's eyes. If she was going to escape, she'd have to act fast.

Tyrone had tight hold on her wrist, pulling her behind him as they ascended the open curving stairway with its paisley carpet runner. Samantha stayed one step behind, the point of her gun jabbing at Isabelle's ribs.

As they topped the final step to the balcony space whose white-painted balusters overlooked the chandelier over the two-story entrance, Samantha must have caught her toe on the rim of the stair or something because she stumbled forward and the gun fell from her hands.

"Oh!"

Samantha's gasp of surprise startled Spiteri, who glanced back and slightly loosened his hold on Isabelle's wrist.

Jerking her arm backward, Isabelle pulled away from Tyrone, in the same motion kicking the gun farther down the stairs. She lunged for the railing, hoping to jump over and maybe even take Samantha out as she went.

Tyrone's thick hands were on her immediately, his grip excruciatingly tight on her shoulders. "You little wench!" He jerked her backward.

Isabelle fought hard, but she was no match for his greater size. Within seconds Samantha had retrieved the gun, and Isabelle stilled her fighting.

"You will cooperate," Tyrone nearly shouted, "or I will kill your family!"

"You don't dare kill my sister," Isabelle reminded him. "And you don't dare kill me, either, so what's the point of having Samantha carry that gun? She knows you'll turn it on her if she shoots me." Isabelle added the last bit for Samantha's benefit. She already knew the ambitious blonde wasn't stupid. Perhaps there was some way to use her assertiveness against Tyrone.

"If I have to kill you and your sister, I will just use Valli as my puppet."

"Valli has been asked to step down as ambassador. He will never be crowned."

"No matter. Stephanos Valli has two younger brothers." Tyrone stopped at the top of the stairs and ran his fingers under Isabelle's chin. "I don't care how I come to rule, but I will come to rule. I liked this plan best, but if you're going to be too difficult, I will kill you. It is as simple as that."

For a fleeting moment, Isabelle considered letting him kill her. It was the only way she could put a stop to his plans.

But, she realized an instant later, Tyrone hadn't gone to all the trouble of the last five days to shoot her now. He was trying to bully her, but he'd underestimated her determination. She, too, had been through a lot in the last five days, and she wasn't the naive schoolgirl he'd attacked two years before. And she'd fought him off then.

And, she decided as the prod of the gun in her back drove her down the hall, she could fight him off again. Her family wasn't dead. She wasn't about to roll over and play dead, either.

Nicolas Grenaldo called Levi while they were en route to the Adirondacks. "The state police are sending an officer. Where do you want him to meet you?"

"*One* officer?" Levi clarified.

"That's all you need. He has got the authority to make the arrest. You boys can do everything else."

Levi realized he should be grateful for that much. "Okay. Tell him to meet us at the riding stable that adjoins Spiteri's property. I'm going to call there next. Thanks."

With only four men in addition to his brother and him, Levi knew they couldn't risk going in guns blazing. He couldn't tell how many men Spiteri might have guarding the place. If they were outnumbered, their only hope would be to take Spiteri by surprise.

At the same time, Levi feared Spiteri might be picking up where he left off with Isabelle. The thought made his insides churn. He had to get to her as quickly as possible—there wasn't a moment to lose. He'd promised to keep her safe. Right now he obviously wasn't doing a very good job.

Levi called the riding stables that bordered Spiteri's estate and got permission to land their helicopter there. When he explained, briefly, that they were hoping to stealthily enter Spiteri's property, the owner, a man named Willie, suggested they hire his horses.

"That would be perfect. Could you have six of them saddled and ready to go in twenty minutes?"

"Sure could," Willie agreed. "This wouldn't have anything to do with a certain Lydian princess who's gone missing, would it?"

Levi sucked in a breath. He knew by calling the stables he risked giving themselves away. What if Willie was friends with Spiteri?

"What makes you ask that?"

"Just that she was engaged to that fellow two years ago. Never could stand the man myself. Couldn't understand what she'd see in a guy like him."

"Yes. You've guessed correctly. We suspect he's holding her prisoner inside the house."

"You know what the house looks like inside?"

"No, I don't."

"My brother had that house built back in '46. I've still got copies of the blueprints in my fire safe. They've redecorated over the years, but I don't think there's ever been a renovation that's moved any walls."

"If you could find those blueprints, Willie, we'd be indebted to you."

"Aw, it's no trouble. You just make sure that girl gets out of there okay."

"I appreciate that. We should be landing in less than fifteen minutes."

Willie gave Levi instructions on how to approach the property through the rugged terrain so as to remain undetected by anyone on Spiteri's wooded estate. Levi thanked him for his help, all the time praying fervently that the man's assistance wasn't too good to be true—and that their conversation hadn't been overheard. If Spiteri had any idea they would be arriving, their mission would be doomed.

No sooner had Levi passed on the news about the horses to his comrades than they came within range of the stable, bringing the helicopter in low, skimming the thick woods until they reached the open paddock where Willie had instructed them to land.

He waved to them from the doorway of the barn. "This way."

Levi and the men hurried to meet him. The rain that had been falling steadily had begun to let up, which Levi was glad for. At his brother's insistence, he'd changed from his wet clothes during the flight, and he wasn't eager to be soaked again.

Willie had blueprints spread out on a desk in the front office of the stable.

"Here's the main entrances," he pointed, quickly running through the layout.

The men already knew they'd be improvising their plan as they discovered what they were up against. There were two main objectives: rescue Isabelle unharmed and capture Spiteri.

Levi didn't know if they could do both, but at the very least, he wanted Isabelle out of there alive. And then he was going to give her that hug he'd wanted to give her before. He'd just have to keep the true depth of his emotions under wraps. But if God saw fit to help him rescue her, he wouldn't complain. To have her in his arms one more time. That's all he was asking for.

Through the open doors of the barn he saw a state police cruiser pull up and come to a stop. Levi darted out the door to greet the officer.

"Thanks for joining us," he greeted the man, trying not to show his disappointment at the man's frail frame and clearly advancing years. All they needed was his authority. They could do the rest.

"Glad to help. Saw on the news about this princess gal." The older officer ambled toward the shelter of the barn and surveyed the men standing around the blueprints. "Looks like you're expecting some resistance."

Levi quickly caught the officer up to speed on the situation with Spiteri.

"So that's the deal then. I can call for some more officers."

Hope rose in Levi's heart. "How soon could they be here?"

"Less than two hours, I'd say."

"But Spiteri may be assaulting the princess even as we speak." Levi hated to admit the truth. He may have failed Isabelle already. "I don't know if we can wait that long."

In spite of the officer's advancing age, he clearly had no problem keeping up with Levi's plans. "If you boys think you can get the job done, you bring him up here. I'll put the cuffs on him. Deal?"

It was the best deal Levi figured he'd get. "Deal." He looked each of his men in the eye in turn and quickly finalized their plans.

The satellite photos his father had procured had shown woods leading up close to the west side of the house. Levi was happy to discover the blueprints revealed the fewest windows on that side of the property. Though it would mean circling out of their way to avoid the cliffs where a creek had cut a small gorge, they could approach from the west, hopefully secure the horses just out of sight in the woods and then split up.

Two would circle around the north side to the garage, where a large service entrance appeared to be the most promising point of entry. The other four would go around to the front of the house, with two stationing themselves just out of sight at the front door and the other two circling back toward the garage from the front, effectively encircling the building.

"Thank you for your help." He nodded to the officer, to Willie, then to his men. "We need to get moving."

Willie had thoughtfully saddled dark colored horses, which would stand out less in the shadowy woods than his whiter horses might. The men headed toward the woods at a canter with Levi and Joe in the lead. When they came within view of the house, Levi dismounted cautiously. His men did the same.

The men had their instructions. There was no reason to speak.

Levi nodded, drew his sidearm and headed for the cover of several broad landscaping bushes that rimmed the corner of the house. From there he leaned against the cool brick and peeked around the corner.

Clear. He gave a nod to his men. Three men followed Joe toward the front of the house. Levi and a man named Greg ducked to avoid being seen through the windows as they ran for the garage. The pattering of gently falling rain helped to conceal the sound of their activity, though the soggy earth was less than ideal and would likely leave telltale footprints.

A voice came out of nowhere. "Do you hear something?"

There was nowhere to hide on the wide-open patio, so Levi sprinted forward, jumping on a guard as he came around the corner. The man crumpled.

"Larry?" Bootsteps echoed on pavement.

Levi dragged Larry's prone figure against the side of the house with a nod to Greg, who stepped up in time to knock the gun out of the air as it preceded its carrier around the corner of the house. Whatever he did next must not have worked so well because when Levi spun around, he saw them engaged in hand-to-hand combat.

The butt of his gun ended their struggle. "Shh," he reminded Greg, who helped him drag the second guard beside Larry. Part of their mission as Sanctuary officers was to do no harm, so they had no intention of killing men who, for all they knew, were innocent other than their choice to work for an unethical employer. But at the same time, they couldn't risk the pair rousing and alerting Spiteri to their presence.

Greg had rope in a fat pouch pocket of his pants, and the two expertly restrained the guards.

Two down. How many more to go?

Levi peeked around the corner. No one coming. He nodded to Greg and they hurried along the wall, stopping to peer around the corner.

A guard stood blinking into an open bay of the garage. He appeared to be talking into an earpiece. "Larry, you're supposed to check in every fifteen minutes. You're two minutes late. Don't make me come back there."

Levi recognized the wire that dangled from the guard's ear—it matched those worn by the guards they'd tied up behind the house. He also saw another man sitting on a lawn chair nearby, an AK-47 balanced across his knees.

Rather than take on both of them, especially when he couldn't see who or what might be hiding in the open garage, Levi ducked back and whispered to Greg. "Two armed guards. One of them is coming around to check on Larry. We take him, then get the next guy when he comes to check on his friend."

Greg nodded and took a couple of steps back.

The point of a gun made the corner first. Levi grabbed the hand that held it, smashing its knuckles against the side of the garage and pulling the gun from the loosened grip before flipping the man over his back. He landed on the ground with a groan.

"Shh." Greg shook his head as he knocked the man out with a kick from his boot.

But it was too late. Levi heard another set of boots pounding pavement.

"Vinni?"

Little as Levi wanted to tangle with the assault rifle, he had no choice. The gun came around the corner, and Levi twisted it sideways as he pulled it from the guard's hands. No sense letting the guy get off a shot. Nothing would give them away like gunfire.

"Hey!" The man yelled as he followed his gun around the corner. Levi planted the butt of the handle between his eyes. The man wavered and dropped.

Greg helped him tie them up. "We're getting low on rope."

With a nod, Levi ducked around the corner and peered into the garage. After circling the SUV and several ATVs parked inside, he reported to Greg. "I found rope. And our guards who accompanied Isabelle, Ralph and Tony. It's tied around them. Untie them and save the rope. We might need it."

"Are you sure it's safe to untie Ralph and Tony?" Greg asked, getting to work on the knots.

"If they were on Tyrone's side, I don't think they'd be tied up."

Silenced by the gags in their mouths, the men nonetheless nodded agreement with Levi's words. Levi left them in Greg's capable hands.

They'd wasted so much time on the guards. It had been hours since Isabelle's message. Levi couldn't wait any longer. He needed inside the house.

* * *

Isabelle balked as Tyrone wrapped thick rope around her ankles. He'd tried to tie her feet to the bedposts the last time they'd been in this room, too. At least he'd let her keep her clothes on thus far, preserving her last shred of dignity. "You don't need to tie me up."

Tyrone only laughed. "Do you think I'm stupid?"

Rather than answer his question directly and risk angering him further, Isabelle kept her mouth shut. Samantha stood in the doorway with the gun pointed their way.

There was no way out. Isabelle blinked back frightened tears as she looked around the room. As she recalled, the second-story windows opened over the paved patio out back. No good to jump from, even if Tyrone hadn't just tightened the knot that held her right ankle to the bed. Thinking and praying hard, Isabelle tried to come up with a way to escape. Nothing.

She looked back at Samantha holding the gun. An instant later the gun flew from Samantha's grip and a hand covered her mouth, pulling her back.

Isabelle gave a tiny gasp.

"What?" Tyrone growled.

"You're—you're tying that awfully tight." She spoke loudly to cover any sound that might come from whatever was happening in the hallway. "Don't you think that's awfully tight?" She kept talking.

She *had* to keep talking. "You don't have to be mean about it, you know. You've already threatened my sister in Milan and my brother in North Africa and my parents in the care of General Lucca."

Isabelle wasn't sure who was in the hallway, but anyone who cared enough to knock Samantha out couldn't be all bad. There was no telling if she'd survive the next few minutes. But she could give whoever was out there information that would help them find her family.

"What's wrong with you?" Tyrone tightened the knot on her other ankle and leaned over her. "I thought you were a classy woman, but now you're screaming like a little girl."

Isabelle couldn't see more than an instant's glimpse of the figure who crept into the room on Tyrone's right side, and she wasn't about to give away the person's presence by trying to get a better look. When she'd fought off Tyrone the last time she'd been in this room, she'd injured his right eye, and he'd gone almost blind on that side.

Whoever was sneaking up on him across the thickly carpeted floor was either aware of the weakness or very, very lucky.

"Tyrone," she tried to think of something she could say to keep his attention, but her mind was nearly frozen with fear. "I think there's something you need to know."

"What could be so important that you have to tell me right now? I think you're just stalling."

"No, this is really important." She focused on keeping her eyes on his, on not looking in the direction from which she'd seen the figure approaching, but what was taking him so long? Had she only imagined someone had come to rescue her? "I think you ought to know that the Lydian laws of succession demand that an heir be a person of faith."

"Faith? That is nonsense. What is your point?"

"Just that if you're going to reign as regent over our child, you'll have to make full confession of your sins, and then everyone would know—"

"That is no problem. I will lie."

He'd hardly spoken the words when he fell with a shudder almost on top of her, and then strong hands pulled him back into a heap on the floor.

Levi!

"What took you so long?" Isabelle whispered as she pulled at the knots that tied her ankles to the bed.

"Shh." Levi pulled out a pocketknife and cut the cords. She clambered from the tall bed with his help and briefly landed against him before stepping over Tyrone's prone figure.

Hurrying to the hall, Isabelle saw a furious-looking Samantha bound and gagged with a guard standing over her.

"Make sure Spiteri doesn't leave," Levi told the guard as he led Isabelle toward the stairs.

They were halfway through the dining room en route to the back kitchen door when the front doors burst open.

"We're under attack!" a uniformed man yelled as he rushed into the foyer.

"I'll get him," the Sanctuary guard waved Levi on as he leapt over the stair rails onto the yelling man.

"Hurry." Levi darted around the dining room table. "Do you know how many men are guarding this place?"

"He always used to have a dozen or so," Isabelle recalled as she scrambled after Levi.

The words were no more than out of her mouth when she heard a ferocious shout echoing through the foyer. Glancing back, she saw the man who'd been guarding Samantha struggling with the uniformed man who'd burst through the front door. And coming down the stairs in a rage, Tyrone Spiteri.

FIFTEEN

Levi pulled Isabelle through the back kitchen door at a run. Greg stood talking to Ralph and Tony as he coiled the rope into a neat ball.

"Spiteri is behind us! Hold him off! Get the 'copter! Do something!" Levi shouted as he sprinted past the men, never letting go of Isabelle's hand.

The helicopter was almost a mile away at the stable. They'd never outrun Spiteri on foot.

"Where are we going?" Isabelle asked as he pulled her toward the woods.

"I have horses up ahead."

He could hear shouting behind him but wouldn't risk looking back. The ground was rugged, the trees unevenly spaced, and one false move could cost them everything. Dark clouds had moved in, bringing with them more rain, and this time, wind and the rumble of thunder.

The horses whinnied a greeting, and the chestnut gelding Levi had ridden earlier pawed the ground eagerly.

For a moment, Levi considered letting Isabelle ride one of the other horses. But he quickly realized that would leave one of his men without a mount. And the slender princess would hardly slow his horse down.

Besides, she already had her shoe through the stirrup and was pulling one jeans-clad leg over. It was all Levi could do to untie the horse and climb on behind her.

"Hah, boy," Isabelle urged the horse on its way, leaning close to the animal's mane.

The high whine of a motor caught Levi's attention, and he looked back in time to see three ATVs peeling out from around the garage. Spiteri rode the one at the head.

"Which way?"

"We've got a helicopter at the riding stables."

Isabelle gave a nod and ducked lower and the horse stretched out. In spite of the trees, the wind and the rain, the animal seemed to have no qualms about running at a full gallop. Well, this was his home turf. And Levi suspected the rumbling thunder may have spooked the animal, sending him running for the safety of his stable.

Fortunately, though the trees tended to be fairly spread out, they grew in such random spots that the wider ATVs had to swerve wide here and there. That, Levi realized, seemed to be their only advantage.

"Hi-yah!" The cry from behind had Levi turning

his head again, and this time he spotted his men on horseback. Three came after the ATVs. He could just see the other two headed toward the open yard and the straightest route to the stables.

Levi felt a burst of hope. If the pilot could reach the helicopter, they would at least have a chance of taking off the moment they reached it. And even a split-second advantage might be all they'd get.

A sudden loud crack sent bits of bark exploding from the nearest tree. At first Levi wasn't sure if it was gunfire or lightning, but a second shot rattled through the leaves near his head, confirming the worst. Spiteri and his men were shooting at them.

Levi reached around Isabelle and pulled the reins to the left, taking them wide around the next tree.

"What are you—" Isabelle began, but as bullet holes appeared in the tree trunk, she quieted her protests. "They're shooting at us?"

"We need to be evasive." Levi pulled the horse to the right. "They won't be too accurate, between the rain and the trees and the fact that they're moving, but it only takes one lucky shot."

"One unlucky shot," Isabelle corrected him, pulling the horse farther to the right.

"Not too far that way. There's a gorge." He warned her.

"I know. But a gorge is better for us than for them. The sides are shallow in a few places. We might be able to make it across. Those ATVs aren't so nimble."

Levi glanced behind them. One of his men had leapt from his horse and was wrestling with a guard on an ATV. Isabelle's plan sounded dangerous, but the other two ATVs were gaining on them. They had little choice.

"All right. Ease closer to the gorge, but be careful. It's difficult to see in this rain."

Lightning shot through the sky somewhere ahead of them as Isabelle guided the horse farther to the right, and the accompanying clap of thunder sent their already-spooked horse rearing back.

From his precarious perch on the back of the saddle, without even so much as a toe through the stirrups, Levi had little else to hold on to but Isabelle as the chestnut gelding pawed the air in terror. Levi wasn't about to risk pulling Isabelle from the horse.

He grabbed for the saddle as he fell backward but found nothing but open air. His back slammed against the wet earth.

"Levi!" Isabelle screamed as the frightened horse shot forward again.

Leaping to his feet, Levi started to run after the horse, but he could hear the ATVs roaring forward just behind him. He ducked behind a tree and tried to catch his breath.

Seconds later an ATV skidded to a stop. Levi

glanced around, hoping to spot some means of escape. There. The gorge was just beyond him.

Darting out from the cover of the tree, Levi ran for the rim of the gorge. Maybe, if he could make it down the bank—

Shots rattled the leaves near his head as he ran. But this time, instead of the engine of the ATV, Levi heard cursing as Spiteri ran after him.

The ground was slick, and rotting leaves clung to his shoes. The edge of the gorge was close, but he quickly saw it was steep at this point, the drop off was sharp and the bottom was out of sight far below.

Suddenly his foot went out from under him and he slid in the wet mud, skidding toward the edge of the ravine. He scrambled to catch hold of something, hoping to avoid a fall from this potentially deadly height, but everything was mud and loose leaves that crumbled to mush as he grabbed at them.

His feet cleared the edge of the gorge.

"Ah-hah!" Spiteri pounced on his chest, slamming the breath from his lungs before hauling him to his feet.

Levi flung himself away from the rim of the cliff, pulling Spiteri down into the mud with him. Tyrone was fumbling with something—his gun. He was attempting to reload the pistol.

With a quick kick, Levi sent the gun flinging out over the gorge. It rattled against the rocks as it fell.

"You idiot!" Spiteri lunged at him.

His hands full of mud and rotting leaves already, Levi shoved the muck toward Spiteri's face, smearing his eyes, which he already knew were the man's weak point.

"Augh!" Spiteri cried, swiping the muck from his face.

Taking advantage of the distraction he'd caused, Levi scrambled through the mud away from the ravine. Through the woods he could see Isabelle guiding the horse back toward him.

"No! Turn back!" He shouted at her. She had to get away. Spiteri was still dangerous.

Glancing back at his enemy, he saw Spiteri pull a gun from a holster near his ankle.

Isabelle was in range!

Levi jumped on Spiteri, grabbing the wrist that held the gun and pushing him back against the tree. He knocked the gun against the rough bark with all his might, but the man's stubborn grip on the gun would not be broken.

Spiteri pulled his knee up into Levi's stomach.

His abs contracted, but he didn't let go of the man's hands. He didn't dare.

"Levi!" Isabelle screamed as the horse drew near.

"Stay back! Get to safety!" he tried to yell at her, but a rumble of thunder cut him off.

As Isabelle and the horse pulled closer, Spiteri got his finger on the trigger and the gun went off, a wild shot into the stormy sky.

The horse reared back, pawing at the air.

Realizing the danger as the hoofs flashed near his face, Levi flung himself to the side, away from the massive striking hoofs.

With a horrible crunching sound, one hoof caught Spiteri in the chest.

The man's face blanched, his ribs likely broken. Then Spiteri twisted himself out from between the tree and the crushing hoof.

He spun back toward the cliff, and for a few seconds wavered between standing and falling. The horse reared again. Spiteri leaned back, away from the pawing hooves and fell over the edge.

Levi launched himself toward the horse. Isabelle had lost hold of the reins and clung to the animal's mane. They were too close to the edge on the slippery soil. Far too close.

Grasping through the air, Levi's fingers found the reins and he pulled the animal back, patting its neck, murmuring soothing sounds to calm the frantic gelding. To his relief, the horse consented to his urging and moved toward safety.

Isabelle slid from the saddle and Levi pulled her into his arms just as the sound of an approaching ATV neared them. Levi turned to block the princess from the oncoming vehicle, but then he recognized Greg piloting the machine.

"Spiteri's men have all been subdued," Greg informed him.

"Excellent. Call Joe—I think he was headed back toward the stables. See if he can get the chopper in here and bring that officer to make the arrest. Spiteri fell down the gorge."

Greg clambered off the ATV and looked over the edge. "He's not moving," he reported.

Relieved, Levi turned his attention to the woman in his arms. Isabelle had buried her face against his shoulder and held him tight.

"Your Majesty?" Levi smoothed back her hair, which had flown wild in the rain and now clung to her cheeks. "Are you all right?"

"I'm all right now."

"Why did you turn back? You could have reached the helicopter by now. You could be safe."

"I couldn't leave you."

"Yes, you could. It's your royal duty—"

"It's my royal duty to protect my people," Isabelle interrupted him. "And I finally figured out how best to do that."

"By running away from help?" he chided her.

"No." Her arms tightened around him, and the press of her warm body against him was more than he could ignore. "By running to you. Spiteri wanted me to marry him to produce an heir. I finally realized the one way I can stop him or anyone else who might try to enact the same plan."

Levi's heart thundered along with the rumbling in the sky nearby. "How's that?"

Her winsome smile as she looked up at him nearly brought him to his knees. "By getting married to someone else first."

The breath left his throat. What did she mean? "You can't—" He shook his head as she nuzzled closer. "Marriage is a serious thing, a covenant between a couple and God. You can't get married just to stop evil from getting the upper hand. It doesn't work that way."

"What if I get married because I'm in love?"

He could feel the blush on her cheeks stealing its way to his. "You—you don't mean—"

She rose up on her tiptoes to kiss him.

It was as wonderful as the kiss they'd shared at the airport. More wonderful, actually.

She pulled away too soon. "I thought so," she whispered.

The gift of speech had left him. "Hmm?"

"You love me, too."

Something wild and strong rose up in his chest. "I have always loved you, Isabelle, and more so every moment I'm with you. But you're a princess."

The corners of her eyes pinched with sadness. "I suppose you've got to stay in this hemisphere?"

A roar above the treetops caught his attention as the helicopter hovered low over the gorge.

"There he is!" Greg shouted, as Joe leaned out the door of the helicopter, the state police officer just visible beyond his elbow. Greg gestured to where Spiteri had fallen. "He hasn't moved."

"Joe!" Levi shouted to his brother.

Joe waved back.

"How would you like to be the president of Sanctuary when Dad retires?"

Joe looked dumbstruck for a moment. "It's all I've ever wanted," he shouted back. "But you're the oldest."

"I've had an offer I can't refuse."

Isabelle giggled and pulled him close.

With a wave, Joe lowered himself down to retrieve Spiteri.

"So, does that mean you're willing to go along with my plan?" the princess asked.

"You've patiently gone along with all my plans, so I suppose it's only fair." He leaned down and kissed her again, until the impatient stomping of the horse reminded him that they were standing outside in the rain, and it would soon be dark.

"We should get you out of the rain." He reached for the horse's reins.

Isabelle held back. "Aren't you forgetting something?"

His mind muddled with emotion, Levi wasn't sure what she meant.

She gave him a patient smile. "The media will want to know what's up. I need something official to tell them."

"Since when do you care what the media want?"
Her only response was an expectant smile.

"Are you sure?" He took a step closer and wrapped one arm around her waist. "So much has happened so quickly. It was only a few days ago you were irritated with me and tried to have me removed from my post as your bodyguard."

"I was irritated because I thought you were cute, and I was sure you were up to something." She brushed a light kiss across his cheek then whispered in his ear, "And I was right. Besides—" she batted her eyes as she looked up at him "—it might be useful having an international law expert in the family. I'm overdue for a mission trip to Africa. Maybe you can pull some strings for me."

"Africa might have to wait until we've found the rest of your family. But then, yes, I think we might make a very good team."

"We already do make a good team." Isabelle looked past him, and Levi turned in time to see Spiteri being raised into the helicopter. It didn't appear as though they'd even tried to make the man comfortable. The older officer clapped the cuffs on him.

A satisfied smile passed over Isabelle's face.

Levi took hold of both her hands before dropping down on one knee.

"Are you all right?" Isabelle gasped.

"Never been better." He smiled up at her. "Princess Isabelle…" He kissed her hand. "Your Highness, would you do me the honor of being my wife?"

Isabelle dropped down onto her knees in the mud beside him. "Yes, yes, yes!" she squealed, covering him with kisses.

"Wait," he protested, trying to help her to her feet while kissing her. "This isn't how it's supposed to go."

"Isn't it?" she giggled as they fell back onto the sodden leaves.

Levi laughed. "All right then, maybe it is." He gave her another kiss, then cradled her face in one palm. "As long as I'm with you."

* * * * *

Dear Reader,

I believe our love for happily-ever-after endings is knit up in our very being, placed there by God himself, because He wanted us to long for that great happily-ever-after which we will inherit when we reach heaven. And I hope that as you endure the less-than-perfect world here, this story will be an encouragement to you, and a reminder that even in the bleakest moments, God is still working out His plan and leading us toward that happy ending.

It has been a joy to spend these pages with you in Lydia. Though Isabelle and Levi have found their happy ending, Lydia is not yet at peace. There is more to come. Please look for the stories of Isabelle's siblings, available through Love Inspired Suspense in the coming months.

Blessings,
Rachelle

Questions for Discussion

1. When the royal motorcade is ambushed, Isabelle is concerned for the safety of her family members. At the same time, she realizes there's nothing she can do at the moment to help them and her duty is to her own safety. Have you ever had to put your own needs before those of the people you loved? How did it make you feel? Do you believe Isabelle made the right choice?

2. Prior to being assigned to guard the princess, Levi had heard about her, was impressed by her character and found her attractive. Under the circumstances, do you think it was a responsible choice for him to become her bodyguard? What were the risks of guarding someone he was attracted to? What benefits might there be?

3. When Princess Isabelle explains her missions work, she says she feels it is her duty as a person of privilege to raise the funds to improve people's lives and to draw public attention to the plight of those in need. What aspects of your life could be leveraged for the benefit of those in need?

4. Levi had always wanted to be president of Sanctuary International when his father retires, and he hopes that by successfully completing this mission, he will earn his father's approval and his job. How do his priorities change over the course of his experiences? Have you ever wanted something very much, only to have your priorities change?

5. Isabelle has been maligned by the media, who call her frigid and unloving. She acknowledges that she could have a public fling and change their perception, but insists that it would be wrong to pretend to be in love with someone just to save her reputation. Do you agree with her choice? What does this show you about her character?

6. Levi hasn't shared much with Isabelle about his job back in New York. Do you think he should have been more forthcoming about his background? Why or why not?

7. When Isabelle sees Levi without his beard, it changes the way she looks at him. Have you ever seen someone in a different light? Was that good or bad for your relationship? What do you think about Isabelle's changing impression of Levi?

8. When they are attacked in the alley, Levi tells Isabelle to go on without him, but she won't leave him. Do you think she made the right choice? How does her choice reveal her growing feelings?

9. Even though Isabelle is afraid of Stephanos Valli, she is determined to return to Lydia and face him if it means increasing the possibility of her family getting to safety. Do you think her choice is wise? What does her decision tell you about her character?

10. Samantha Klein was rejected by Levi years before. How do you think her feelings play into her choices later in the story? Have you ever been betrayed by anyone? Do you believe Samantha's choices were Levi's fault?

11. Stephanos Valli claims to be a pawn in the hands of more powerful people. Do you believe he is telling the truth?

12. Levi and Isabelle aren't sure if they can trust Sergio Cana, but they accept the key he gave them. Have you ever been unsure if someone could be trusted? Did your feelings of distrust influence the choices you made?

13. As Isabelle is investigating the three generals, Levi warns her that she might learn unpleasant things about her own father, who trusted the generals and worked with them on a regular basis. Isabelle acknowledges that her father may have made compromises before. Have you ever been pressured to compromise your convictions? How does the tangled web Isabelle discovers influence her willingness to compromise? Do you think the ambush is related to King Philip's previous choices?

14. As Levi falls more in love with Isabelle, he feels he must send her away, not only for her own safety, but also to keep from becoming further involved with her. Do you think he acted honorably in doing so? What might he have done differently?

15. Levi and Isabelle haven't known each other for a very long time when they become engaged. How do the intensity of their experiences compensate for the short time they've know each other? Do you think their love will last?

LARGER-PRINT BOOKS!

**GET 2 FREE
LARGER-PRINT NOVELS
PLUS 2 FREE
MYSTERY GIFTS**

Love Inspired

SUSPENSE
RIVETING INSPIRATIONAL ROMANCE

Larger-print novels are now available...

YES! Please send me 2 FREE LARGER-PRINT Love Inspired® Suspense novels and my 2 FREE mystery gifts (gifts are worth about $10). After receiving them, if I don't wish to receive any more books, I can return the shipping statement marked "cancel". If I don't cancel, I will receive 4 brand-new novels every month and be billed just $4.99 per book in the U.S. or $5.49 per book in Canada. That's a saving of at least 23% off the cover price. It's quite a bargain! Shipping and handling is just 50¢ per book in the U.S. and 75¢ per book in Canada.* I understand that accepting the 2 free books and gifts places me under no obligation to buy anything. I can always return a shipment and cancel at any time. Even if I never buy another book, the two free books and gifts are mine to keep forever.

110/310 IDN FEH3

Name _____ (PLEASE PRINT) _____

Address _____ Apt. # _____

City _____ State/Prov. _____ Zip/Postal Code _____

Signature (if under 18, a parent or guardian must sign)

Mail to the Reader Service:
IN U.S.A.: P.O. Box 1867, Buffalo, NY 14240-1867
IN CANADA: P.O. Box 609, Fort Erie, Ontario L2A 5X3

Not valid for current subscribers to Love Inspired Suspense larger-print books.

**Are you a current subscriber to Love Inspired Suspense books
and want to receive the larger-print edition?
Call 1-800-873-8635 or visit www.ReaderService.com.**

* Terms and prices subject to change without notice. Prices do not include applicable taxes. Sales tax applicable in N.Y. Canadian residents will be charged applicable taxes. Offer not valid in Quebec. This offer is limited to one order per household. All orders subject to credit approval. Credit or debit balances in a customer's account(s) may be offset by any other outstanding balance owed by or to the customer. Please allow 4 to 6 weeks for delivery. Offer available while quantities last.

Your Privacy—The Reader Service is committed to protecting your privacy. Our Privacy Policy is available online at www.ReaderService.com or upon request from the Reader Service.

We make a portion of our mailing list available to reputable third parties that offer products we believe may interest you. If you prefer that we not exchange your name with third parties, or if you wish to clarify or modify your communication preferences, please visit us at www.ReaderService.com/consumerschoice or write to us at Reader Service Preference Service, P.O. Box 9062, Buffalo, NY 14269. Include your complete name and address.

LISUSLP11B

LARGER-PRINT BOOKS!

GET 2 FREE
LARGER-PRINT NOVELS
PLUS 2 FREE
MYSTERY GIFTS

Love Inspired

Larger-print novels are now available...